Stories By English Authors In France

Stories By English Authors In France
Various Authors

PO Box 2211
Fairfield, IA 52556
www.1stworldlibrary.org
First Edition

LCCN: 2003195156

ISBN: 1-59540-528-3

Purchase *"Stories By English Authors In France"*
as a traditional bound book at:
www.1stWorldLibrary.org/purchase.asp?ISBN=1-59540-528-3

1st World Library Literary Society is a nonprofit organization dedicated to promoting literacy by:

- Creating a free internet library accessible from any computer worldwide.
- Hosting writing competitions and offering book publishing scholarships.

Readers interested in supporting literacy through sponsorship, donations or membership please contact:
literacy@1stworldlibrary.org
Check us out at: www.1stworldlibrary.org

Stories By English Authors In France

contributed by the Charles Family

in support of

1st World Library Literary Society

Contents

A LODGING FOR THE NIGHT

It was late in November, 1456. The snow fell over Paris with rigorous, relentless persistence; sometimes the wind made a sally and scattered it in flying vortices; sometimes there was a lull, and flake after flake descended out of the black night air, silent, circuitous, interminable. To poor people, looking up under moist eyebrows, it seemed a wonder where it all came from. Master Francis Villon had propounded an alternative that afternoon, at a tavern window: was it only pagan Jupiter plucking geese upon Olympus? or were the holy angels moulting? He was only a poor Master of Arts, he went on; and as the question somewhat touched upon divinity, he durst not venture to conclude. A silly old priest from Montargis, who was among the company, treated the young rascal to a bottle of wine in honour of the jest and grimaces with which it was accompanied, and swore on his own white beard that he had been just such another irreverent dog when he was Villon's age.

The air was raw and pointed, but not far below freezing; and the flakes were large, damp, and adhesive. The whole city was sheeted up. An army might have marched from end to end and not a footfall given the alarm. If there were any belated birds in heaven, they saw the island like a large white patch, and the bridges like slim white spars on the black ground of the river. High up overhead the snow settled among the tracery of the cathedral towers. Many a niche was drifted full; many a statue wore a long white bonnet on its grotesque or sainted head. The gargoyles had been transformed into great false noses, drooping toward the point. The crockets were like upright pillows swollen on one side. In the intervals of the wind there was a dull sound dripping about the precincts of the church.

The cemetery of St. John had taken its own share of the snow. All the graves were decently covered; tall white housetops stood around in grave array; worthy burghers were long ago in bed, be-nightcapped like their domiciles; there was no light in all the neighbourhood but a little peep from a lamp that hung swinging in the church choir, and tossed the shadows to and fro in time to its oscillations. The clock was hard on ten when the patrol went by with halberds and a lantern, beating their hands; and they saw nothing suspicious about the cemetery of St. John.

Yet there was a small house, backed up against the cemetery wall, which was still awake, and awake to evil purpose, in that snoring district. There was not much to betray it from without; only a stream of warm vapour from the chimney-top, a patch where the snow melted on the roof, and a few half-obliterated footprints at the door. But within, behind the shuttered windows, Master Francis Villon, the poet, and some of the thievish crew with whom he consorted, were keeping the night alive and passing round the bottle.

A great pile of living embers diffused a strong and ruddy glow from the arched chimney. Before this straddled Dom Nicolas, the Picardy monk, with his skirts picked up and his fat legs bared to the comfortable warmth. His dilated shadow cut the room in half; and the firelight only escaped on either side of his broad person, and in a little pool between his outspread feet. His face had the beery, bruised appearance of the continual drinker's; it was covered with a network of congested veins, purple in ordinary circumstances, but now pale violet, for even with his back to the fire the cold pinched him on the other side. His cowl had half fallen back, and made a strange excrescence on either side of his bull-neck. So he straddled, grumbling, and cut the room in half with the shadow of his portly frame.

On the right, Villon and Guy Tabary were huddled together over a scrap of parchment; Villon making a ballade which he was to call the "Ballade of Roast Fish," and Tabary sputtering admiration at his shoulder. The poet was a rag of a man, dark, little, and lean, with hollow cheeks and thin black locks. He carried his four and twenty years with feverish animation. Greed had made folds about his eyes, evil smiles had puckered his mouth. The wolf and pig struggled together in his face. It was an eloquent, sharp, ugly, earthly countenance. His hands were small and prehensile, with fingers knotted like a cord; and they were continually flickering in front of him in violent and expressive pantomime. As for Tabary, a broad, complacent, admiring imbecility breathed from his squash nose and slobbering lips; he had become a thief, just as he might have become the most decent of burgesses, by the imperious chance that rules the lives of human geese and human donkeys.

At the monk's other hand, Montigny and Thevenin Pensete played a game of chance. About the first there clung some flavour of good birth and training, as about a fallen angel; something long, lithe, and courtly in the person; something aquiline and darkling in the face. Thevenin, poor soul, was in great feather; he had done a good stroke of knavery that afternoon in the Faubourg St. Jacques, and all night he had been gaining from Montigny. A flat smile illuminated his face; his bald head shone rosily in a garland of red curls; his little protuberant stomach shook with silent chucklings as he swept in his gains.

"Doubles or quits?" said Thevenin.

Montigny nodded grimly.

"Some may prefer to dine in state," wrote Villon, "on bread and cheese on silver plate. Or, or - help me out, Guido!"

Tabary giggled.

"Or parsley on a golden dish," scribbled the poet.

The wind was freshening without; it drove the snow before it, and sometimes raised its voice in a victorious whoop, and made sepulchral grumblings in the chimney. The cold was growing sharper as the night went on. Villon, protruding his lips, imitated the gust with something between a whistle and a groan. It was an eerie, uncomfortable talent of the poet's, much detested by the Picardy monk.

"Can't you hear it rattle in the gibbet?" said Villon. "They are all dancing the devil's jig on nothing, up there. You may dance, my gallants; you'll be none the warmer. Whew, what a gust! Down went somebody just now! A medlar the fewer on the three-legged medlar-tree! I say, Dom Nicolas, it'll be cold to-night on the St. Denis Road?" he asked.

Dom Nicholas winked both his big eyes, and seemed to choke upon his Adam's apple. Montfaucon, the great, grisly Paris gibbet, stood hard by the St. Denis Road, and the pleasantry touched him on the raw. As for Tabary, he laughed immoderately over the medlars; he had never heard anything more light-hearted; and he held his sides and crowed. Villon fetched him a fillip on the nose, which turned his mirth into an attack of coughing.

"Oh, stop that row," said Villon, "and think of rhymes to 'fish'!"

"Doubles or quits? Said Montigny, doggedly.

"With all my heart," quoth Thevenin.

"Is there any more in that bottle?" asked the monk.

"Open another," said Villon. "How do you ever hope to fill that big hogshead, your body, with little things like bottles? And how do you expect to get to heaven? How many angels, do you fancy, can be spared to carry up a single monk from Picardy? Or do you think yourself another Elias - and they'll send the coach for you?"

"Hominibus impossible," replied the monk, as he filled his glass.

Tabary was in ecstasies.

Villon filliped his nose again.

"Laugh at my jokes, if you like," he said.

Villon made a face at him. "Think of rhymes to 'fish,' " he said. "What have you to do with Latin? You'll wish you knew none of it at the great assizes, when the devil calls for Guido Tabary, clericus - the devil with the humpback and red-hot fingernails. Talking of the devil," he added, in a whisper, "look at Montigny!"

All three peered covertly at the gamester. He did not seem to be enjoying his luck. His mouth was a little to a side; one nostril nearly shut, and the other much inflated. The black dog was on his back, as people say, in terrifying nursery metaphor; and he breathed hard under the gruesome burden.

"He looks as if he could knife him," whispered Tabary, with round eyes.

The monk shuddered, and turned his face and spread his open hands to the red embers. It was the cold that thus affected Dom Nicolas, and not any excess of moral sensibility.

"Come now," said Villon - "about this ballade. How does it run so far?" And beating time with his hand, he read it aloud to Tabary.

They were interrupted at the fourth rhyme by a brief and fatal movement among the gamesters. The round was completed, and Thevenin was just opening his mouth to claim another victory, when Montigny leaped up, swift as an adder, and stabbed him to the heart. The blow took effect before he had time to utter a cry, before he had time to move. A tremor or two convulsed his frame; his hands opened and shut, his heels rattled on the floor; then his head rolled backward over one shoulder, with eyes wide open; and Thevenin Pensete's spirit had returned to Him who made it.

Every one sprang to his feet; but the business was over in two twos. The four living fellows looked at each other in rather a ghastly fashion, the dead man contemplating a corner of the roof with a singular and ugly leer.

"My God!" said Tabary, and he began to pray in Latin.

Villon broke out into hysterical laughter. He came a step forward and ducked a ridiculous bow at Thevenin, and laughed still louder. Then he sat down suddenly, all of a heap, upon a stool, and continued laughing bitterly, as though he would shake himself to pieces.

Montigny recovered his composure first.

"Let's see what he has about him," he remarked; and he picked the dead man's pockets with a practised hand, and divided the money into four equal portions on the table. "There's for you," he said.

The monk received his share with a deep sigh, and a single stealthy glance at the dead Thevenin, who was beginning to sink into himself and topple sideways off the chair.

"We're all in for it," cried Villon, swallowing his mirth. "It's a hanging job for every man Jack of us that's here - not to speak of those who aren't." He made a shocking gesture in the air with his raised right hand, and put out his tongue and threw his head on one side, so as to counterfeit the appearance of one who has been hanged. Then he pocketed his share of the spoil, and executed a shuffle with his feet as if to restore the circulation.

Tabary was the last to help himself; he made a dash at the money, and retired to the other end of the apartment.

Montigny stuck Thevenin upright in the chair, and drew out the dagger, which was followed by a jet of blood.

"You fellows had better be moving," he said, as he wiped the blade on his victim's doublet.

"I think we had," returned Villon, with a gulp. "Damn his fat head!" he broke out. "It sticks in my throat like phlegm. What right has a man to have red hair when he is dead?" And he fell all of a heap again upon the stool, and fairly covered his face with his hands.

Montigny and Dom Nicolas laughed aloud, even Tabary feebly chiming in.

"Cry-baby!" said the monk.

"I always said he was a woman," added Montigny, with a sneer. "Sit up, can't you?" he went on, giving another shake to the murdered body. "Tread out that fire, Nick!"

But Nick was better employed; he was quietly taking Villon's purse, as the poet sat, limp and trembling, on the stool where he had been making a ballade not three minutes before. Montigny and Tabary dumbly demanded a share of the booty, which the monk silently promised as he passed the little bag into the bosom of his gown. In many ways an artistic nature unfits a man for practical existence.

No sooner had the theft been accomplished than Villon shook himself, jumped to his feet, and began helping to scatter and extinguish the embers. Meanwhile Montigny opened the door and cautiously peered into the street. The coast was clear; there was no meddlesome patrol in sight. Still it was judged wiser to slip out severally; and as Villon was himself in a hurry to escape from the neighbourhood of the dead Thevenin, and the rest were in a still greater hurry to get rid of him before he should discover the loss of his money, he was the first by general consent to issue forth into the street.

The wind had triumphed and swept all the clouds from heaven. Only a few vapours, as thin as moonlight, fleeted rapidly across the stars. It was bitter cold; and, by a common optical effect, things seemed almost more definite than in the broadest daylight. The sleeping city was absolutely still; a company of white hoods, a field full of little alps, below the twinkling stars. Villon cursed his fortune. Would it were still snowing! Now, wherever he went, he left an indelible trail behind him on the glittering streets; wherever he went, he was still tethered to the house by the cemetery of St. John; wherever he went, he must weave, with his own plodding feet, the rope that bound him to the crime and would bind him to the gallows. The leer of the dead man came back to him with new significance. He snapped his fingers as if to pluck up his own spirits, and, choosing a street at random, stepped boldly forward in the snow.

Two things preoccupied him as he went: the aspect of the gallows at Montfaucon in this bright, windy phase of the night's existence, for one; and for another, the look of the dead man with his bald head and garland of red curls. Both struck cold upon his heart, and he kept quickening his pace as if he could escape from unpleasant thoughts by mere fleetness of foot. Sometimes he looked back over his shoulder with a sudden nervous jerk; but he was the only moving thing in the white streets, except when the wind swooped round a corner and threw up the snow, which was beginning to freeze, in spouts of glittering dust.

Suddenly he saw, a long way before him, a black clump and a couple of lanterns. The clump was in motion, and the lanterns swung as though carried by men walking. It was a patrol. And though it was merely crossing his line of march he judged it wiser to get out of eyeshot as speedily as he could. He was not in the humour to be challenged, and he was conscious of making a very conspicuous mark upon the snow. Just on his left hand there stood a great hotel, with some turrets and a large porch before the door; it was half ruinous, he remembered, and had long stood empty; and so he made three steps of it, and jumped into the shelter of the porch. It was pretty dark inside, after the glimmer of the snowy streets, and he was groping forward with outspread hands, when he stumbled over some substance which offered an indescribable mixture of resistances, hard and soft, firm and loose. His heart gave a leap, and he sprang two steps back and stared dreadfully at the obstacle. Then he gave a little laugh of relief. It was only a woman, and she dead. He knelt beside her to make sure upon this latter point. She was freezing cold, and rigid like a stick. A little ragged finery fluttered in the wind about her hair, and her cheeks had been heavily rouged that same afternoon. Her pockets were quite empty; but in her stocking, underneath the garter, Villon found two of the small coins that went by the name of whites. It was little enough, but it was always something; and the poet was moved with a deep sense of pathos that she should have died before she had spent her money. That seemed to him a dark and pitiable mystery; and he looked from the coins in his hand to the dead woman, and back again to the coins, shaking his head over the riddle of man's life. Henry V. of England, dying at Vincennes just after he had conquered France, and this poor jade cut off by a cold draught in a great man's doorway before she had time to spend her couple of whites - it seemed a cruel way to carry on the world. Two whites would have taken such a little while to squander; and yet it would have been one more good taste in the mouth, one more smack of the lips, before the devil got the soul, and the body was left to birds and vermin. He would like to use all his tallow before the light was blown out and the lantern broken.

While these thoughts were passing through his mind, he was feeling, half mechanically, for his purse. Suddenly his heart stopped beating; a feeling of cold scales passed up the back of his legs, and a cold blow seemed to fall upon his scalp. He stood petrified for a moment; then he felt again with one feverish movement; then his loss burst upon him, and he was covered at once with perspiration. To spendthrifts money is so living and actual - it is such a thin veil between them and their pleasures! There is only one limit to their fortune - that of time; and a spendthrift with only a few crowns is the Emperor of Rome until they are spent. For such a person to lose his money is to suffer the most shocking reverse, and fall from heaven to hell, from all to nothing, in a breath. And all the more if he has put his head in the halter for it; if he may be hanged to-morrow for that same purse, so dearly earned, so foolishly departed! Villon stood and cursed; he threw the two whites into the street; he shook his fist at heaven; he stamped, and was not horrified to find himself trampling the poor corpse. Then he began rapidly to retrace his steps toward the house beside the cemetery. He had forgotten all fear of the patrol, which was long gone by at any rate, and had no idea but that of his lost purse. It was in vain that he looked right and left upon the snow; nothing was to be seen. He had not dropped it in the streets. Had it fallen in the house? He would have liked dearly to go in and see; but the idea of the grisly occupant unmanned him. And he saw besides, as he drew near, that their efforts to put out the fire had been unsuccessful; on the contrary, it had broken into a blaze, and a changeful light played in the chinks of door and window, and revived his terror for the authorities and Paris gibbet.

He returned to the hotel with the porch, and groped about upon the snow for the money he had thrown way in his childish passion. But he could only find one white; the other had probably struck sideways and sunk deeply in. With a single white in his pocket, all his projects for a rousing night in some wild tavern vanished utterly away. And it was not only pleasure that fled laughing from his grasp; positive discomfort, positive pain, attacked him as he stood ruefully before the porch. His perspiration had dried upon him; and although the wind had now fallen, a binding frost was setting in stronger with every hour, and he felt benumbed and sick at heart. What was to be done? Late as was the hour, improbable as was his success, he would try the house of his adopted father, the chaplain of St. Benoit.

He ran all the way, and knocked timidly. There was no answer. He knocked again and again, taking heart with every stroke; and at last steps were heard approaching from within. A barred wicket fell open in the iron-studded door, and emitted a gush of yellow light.

"Hold up your face to the wicket," said the chaplain from within.

"It's only me," whimpered Villon.

"Oh, it's only you, is it?" returned the chaplain; and he cursed him with foul, unpriestly oaths for disturbing him at such an hour, and bade him be off to hell, where he came from.

"My hands are blue to the wrist," pleaded Villon; "my feet are dead and full of twinges; my nose aches with the sharp air; the cold lies at my heart. I may be dead before morning. Only this once, father, and, before God, I will never ask again!"

"You should have come earlier," said the ecclesiastic, coolly. "Young men require a lesson now and then." He shut the wicket and retired deliberately into the interior of the house.

Villon was beside himself; he beat upon the door with his hands and feet, and shouted hoarsely after the chaplain.

"Wormy old fox!" he cried. "If I had my hand under your twist, I would send you flying headlong into the bottomless pit."

A door shut in the interior, faintly audible to the poet down long passages. He passed his hand over his mouth with an oath. And then the humour of the situation struck him, and he laughed and looked lightly up to heaven, where the stars seemed to be winking over his discomfiture.

What was to be done? It looked very like a night in the frosty streets. The idea of the dead woman popped into his imagination, and gave him a hearty fright; what had happened to her in the early night might very well happen to him before morning. And he so young! And with such immense possibilities of disorderly amusement before him! He felt quite pathetic over the notion of his own fate, as if it had been some one else's, and made a little imaginative vignette of the scene in the morning when they should find his body.

He passed all his chances under review, turning the white between his thumb and forefinger. Unfortunately he was on bad terms with some old friends who would once have taken pity on him in such a plight. He had lampooned them in verses; he had beaten and cheated them; and yet now, when he was in so close a pinch, he thought there was at least one who might perhaps relent. It was a chance. It was worth trying at least, and he would go and see.

On the way, two little accidents happened to him which coloured his musings in a very different manner. For, first, he fell in with the track of a patrol, and walked in it for some hundred yards, although it lay out of his direction. And this spirited him up; at least he had confused his trail; for he was still possessed with the idea of people tracking him all about Paris over the snow, and collaring him next morning before he was awake. The other matter affected him quite differently. He passed a street-corner where, not so long before, a woman and her child had been devoured by wolves. This was just the kind of weather, he reflected, when wolves might take it into their heads to enter Paris again; and a lone man in these deserted streets would run the chance of something worse than a mere scare. He stopped and looked upon the place with an unpleasant interest - it was a centre where several lanes intersected each other; and he looked down them all, one after another, and held his breath to listen, lest he should detect some galloping black things on the snow or hear the sound of howling between him and the river. He remembered his mother telling him the story and pointing out the spot, while he was yet a child. His mother! If he only knew where she lived, he might make sure at least of shelter. He determined he would inquire upon the morrow; nay, he would go and see her, too, poor old girl! So thinking, he arrived at his destination - his last hope for the night.

The house was quite dark, like its neighbours; and yet after a few taps he heard a movement overhead, a door opening, and a cautious voice asking who was there. The poet named himself in a loud whisper, and waited, not without some trepidation, the result. Nor had he to wait long. A window was suddenly opened, and a pailful of slops splashed down upon the door-step. Villon had not been unprepared for something of the sort, and had put himself as much in shelter as the nature of the porch admitted; but for all that he was deplorably drenched below the waist. His hose began to freeze almost at once. Death from cold and exposure stared him in the face; he remembered he was of phthisical tendency, and began coughing tentatively. But the gravity of the danger steadied his nerves. He stopped a few hundred yards from the door where he had been so rudely used, and reflected with his finger to his nose. He could only see one way of getting a lodging, and that was to take it. He had noticed a house not far away, which looked as if it might be easily broken into; and thither he betook himself promptly, entertaining himself on the way with the idea of a room still hot, with a table still loaded with the remains of supper, where he might pass the rest of the black hours, and whence he should issue, on the morrow, with an armful of valuable plate. He even considered on what viands and what wines he should prefer; and as he was calling the roll of his favourite dainties, roast fish presented itself to his mind with an odd mixture of amusement and horror.

"I shall never finish that ballade," he thought to himself; and then, with another shudder at the recollection, "Oh, damn his fat head!" he repeated, fervently, and spat upon the snow.

The house in question looked dark at first sight; but as Villon made a preliminary inspection in search of the handiest point of attack, a little twinkle of light caught his eye from behind a curtained window.

"The devil!" he thought. "People awake! Some student or some saint, confound the crew! Can't they get drunk and lie in bed snoring like their neighbours? What's the good of curfew, and poor devils of bell-ringers jumping at a rope's end in bell-towers? What's the use of day, if people sit up all night? The gripes to them!" He grinned as he saw where his logic was leading him. "Every man to his business, after all," added he, "and if they're awake, by the Lord, I may come by a supper honestly for once, and cheat the devil."

He went boldly to the door and knocked with an assured hand. On both previous occasions he had knocked timidly and with some dread of attracting notice; but now when he had just discarded the thought of a burglarious entry, knocking at a door seemed a mighty simple and innocent proceeding. The sound of his blows echoed through the house with thin, phantasmal reverberations, as though it were quite empty; but these had scarcely died away before a measured tread drew near, a couple of bolts were withdrawn, and one wing was opened broadly, as though no guile or fear of guile were known to those within. A tall figure of a man, muscular and spare, but a little bent, confronted Villon. The head was massive in bulk, but finely sculptured; the nose blunt at the bottom, but refining upward to where it joined a pair of strong and honest eyebrows; the mouth and eyes surrounded with delicate markings; and the whole face based upon a thick white beard, boldly and squarely trimmed. Seen as it was by the light of a flickering hand-lamp, it looked perhaps nobler than it had a right to do; but it was a fine face, honourable rather than intelligent, strong, simple, and righteous.

"You knock late, sir," said the old man, in resonant, courteous tones.

Villon cringed, and brought up many servile words of apology; at a crisis of this sort, the beggar was uppermost in him, and the man of genius hid his head with confusion.

"You are cold," repeated the old man, "and hungry?

Well, step in." And he ordered him into the house with a noble enough gesture.

"Some great seigneur," thought Villon, as his host, setting down the lamp on the flagged pavement of the entry, shot the bolts once more into their places.

"You will pardon me if I go in front," he said, when this was done; and he preceded the poet upstairs into a large apartment, warmed with a pan of charcoal and lit by a great lamp hanging from the roof. It was very bare of furniture; only some gold plate on a sideboard, some folios, and a stand of armour between the windows. Some smart tapestry hung upon the walls, representing the crucifixion of our Lord in one piece, and in another a scene of shepherds and shepherdesses by a running stream. Over the chimney was a shield of arms.

"Will you seat yourself," said the old man, "and forgive me if I leave you? I am alone in my house to-night, and if you are to eat I must forage for you myself."

No sooner was his host gone than Villon leaped from the chair on which he had just seated himself, and began examining the room with the stealth and passion of a cat. He weighed the gold flagons in his hand, opened all the folios, and investigated the arms upon the shield, and the stuff with which the seats were lined. He raised the window curtains, and saw that the windows were set with rich stained glass in figures, so far as he could see, of martial import. Then he stood in the middle of the room, drew a long breath, and retaining it with puffed cheeks, looked round and round him, turning on his heels, as if to impress every feature of the apartment on his memory.

"Seven pieces of plate," he said. "If there had been ten, I would have risked it. A fine house, and a fine old master, so help me all the saints!"

And just then, hearing the old man's tread returning along the corridor, he stole back to his chair, and began humbly toasting his wet legs before the charcoal pan.

His entertainer had a plate of meat in one hand and a jug of wine in the other. He set down the plate upon the table, motioning Villon to draw in his chair, and going to the sideboard, brought back two goblets, which he filled.

"I drink your better fortune," he said gravely, touching Villon's cup with his own.

"To our better acquaintance," said the poet, growing bold. A mere man of the people would have been awed by the courtesy of the old seigneur, but Villon was hardened in that matter; he had made mirth for great lords before now, and found them as black rascals as himself. And so he devoted himself to the viands with a ravenous gusto, while the old man, leaning backward, watched him with steady, curious eyes.

"You have blood on your shoulder, my man," he said.

Montigny must have laid his wet right hand upon him as he left the house. He cursed Montigny in his heart.

"It was none of my shedding," he stammered.

"I had not supposed so," returned his host, quietly. "A brawl?"

"Well, something of that sort," Villon admitted, with a quaver.

"Perhaps a fellow murdered?"

"Oh no, not murdered," said the poet, more and more confused. "It was all fair play - murdered by accident. I had no hand in it, God strike me dead!" he added, fervently.

"One rogue the fewer, I dare say," observed the master of the house.

"You may dare to say that," agreed Villon, infinitely relieved. "As big a rogue as there is between here and Jerusalem. He turned up his toes like a lamb. But it was a nasty thing to look at. I dare say you've seen dead men in your time, my lord?" he added, glancing at the armour.

"Many," said the old man. "I have followed the wars, as you imagine."

Villon laid down his knife and fork, which he had just taken up again.

"Were any of them bald?" he asked.

"Oh yes, and with hair as white as mine."

"I don't think I should mind the white so much," said Villon. "His was red." And he had a return of his shuddering and tendency to laughter, which he drowned with a great draught of wine. "I'm a little put out when I think of it," he went on. "I knew him - damn him! And then the cold gives a man fancies - or the fancies give a man cold, I don't know which."

"Have you any money?" asked the old man.

"I have one white," returned the poet, laughing. "I got it out of a dead jade's stocking in a porch. She was as dead as Caesar, poor wench, and as cold as a church, with bits of ribbon sticking in her hair. This is a hard winter for wolves and wenches and poor rogues like me."

"I," said the old man, "am Enguerrand de la Feuillee, seigneur de Brisetout, bailie du Patatrac. Who and what may you be?"

Villon rose and made a suitable reverence. "I am called Francis Villon," he said, "a poor Master of Arts of this university. I know some Latin, and a deal of vice. I can make Chansons, ballades, lais, virelais, and roundels, and I am very fond of wine. I was born in a garret, and I shall not improbably die upon the gallows. I may add, my lord, that from this night forward I am your lordship's very obsequious servant to command."

"No servant of mine," said the knight. "My guest for this evening, and no more."

"A very grateful guest," said Villon, politely, and he drank in dumb show to his entertainer.

"You are shrewd," began the old man, tapping his forehead, "very shrewd; you have learning; you are a clerk; and yet you take a small piece of money off a dead woman in the street. Is it not a kind of theft?"

"It is a kind of theft much practised in the wars, my lord."

"The wars are the field of honour," returned the old man, proudly. "There a man plays his life upon the cast; he fights in the name of his lord the king, his Lord God, and all their lordships the holy saints and angels."

"Put it," said Villon, "that I were really a thief, should I not play my life also, and against heavier odds?"

"For gain, but not for honour."

"Gain?" repeated Villon, with a shrug. "Gain! The poor fellow wants supper, and takes it. So does the soldier in a campaign. Why, what are all these requisitions we hear so much about? If they are not gain to those who take them, they are loss enough to the others. The men-at-arms drink by a good fire, while the burgher bites his nails to buy them wine and wood. I have seen a good many ploughmen swinging on trees about the country; ay, I have seen thirty on one elm, and a very poor figure they made; and when I asked some one how all these came to be hanged, I was told it was because they could not scrape together enough crowns to satisfy the men-at-arms."

"These things are a necessity of war, which the low-born must endure with constancy. It is true that some captains drive overhard; there are spirits in every rank not easily moved by pity; and indeed many follow arms who are no better than brigands."

"You see," said the poet, "you cannot separate the soldier from the brigand; and what is a thief but an isolated brigand with circumspect manners? I steal a couple of mutton-chops, without so much as disturbing people's sleep; the farmer grumbles a bit, but sups none the less wholesomely on what remains. You come up blowing gloriously on a trumpet, take away the whole sheep, and beat the farmer pitifully into the bargain. I have no trumpet; I am only Tom, Dick, or Harry; I am a rogue and a dog, and hanging's too good for me - with all my heart; but just ask the farmer which of us he prefers, just find out which of us he lies awake to curse on cold nights."

"Look at us two," said his lordship. "I am old, strong, and honoured. If I were turned from my house to-morrow, hundreds would be proud to shelter me. Poor people would go out and pass the night in the streets with their children, if I merely hinted that I wished to be alone. And I find you up, wandering homeless, and picking farthings off dead women by the wayside! I fear no man and nothing; I have seen you tremble and lose countenance at a word. I wait God's summons contentedly in my own house, or, if it please the king to call me out again, upon the field of battle. You look for the gallows; a rough, swift death, without hope or honour. Is there no difference between these two?"

"As far as to the moon," Villon acquiesced. "But if I had been born lord of Brisetout, and you had been the poor scholar Francis, would the difference have been any the less? Should not I have been warming my knees at this charcoal pan, and would not you have been groping for farthings in the snow? Should not I have been the soldier, and you the thief?"

"A thief?" cried the old man. "I a thief! If you understood your words, you would repent them."

Villon turned out his hands with a gesture of inimitable impudence. "If your lordship had done me the honour to follow my argument!" he said.

"I do you too much honour in submitting to your presence," said the knight. "Learn to curb your tongue when you speak with old and honourable men, or some one hastier than I may reprove you in a sharper fashion." And he rose and paced the lower end of the apartment, struggling with anger and antipathy. Villon surreptitiously refilled his cup, and settled himself more comfortably in the chair, crossing his knees and leaning his head upon one hand and the elbow against the back of the chair. He was now replete and warm; and he was in no wise frightened for his host, having gauged him as justly as was possible between two such different characters. The night was far spent, and in a very comfortable fashion after all; and he felt morally certain of a safe departure on the morrow.

"Tell me one thing," said the old man, pausing in his walk. "Are you really a thief?"

"I claim the sacred rights of hospitality," returned the poet. "My lord, I am."

"You are very young," the knight continued.

"I should never have been so old," replied Villon, showing his fingers, "if I had not helped myself with these ten talents. They have been my nursing mothers and my nursing fathers."

"You may still repent and change."

"I repent daily," said the poet. "There are few people

more given to repentance than poor Francis. As for change, let somebody change my circumstances. A man must continue to eat, if it were only that he may continue to repent."

"The change must begin in the heart," returned the old man, solemnly.

"My dear lord," answered Villon, "do you really fancy that I steal for pleasure? I hate stealing, like any other piece of work or of danger. My teeth chatter when I see a gallows. But I must eat, I must drink; I must mix in society of some sort. What the devil! Man is not a solitary animal - cui Deus foeminam tradit. Make me king's pantler, make me Abbot of St. Denis, make me bailie of the Patatrac, and then I shall be changed indeed. But as long as you leave me the poor scholar Francis Villon, without a farthing, why, of course, I remain the same."

"The grace of God is all powerful."

"I should be a heretic to question it," said Francis. "It has made you lord of Brisetout and bailie of the Patatrac; it has given me nothing but the quick wits under my hat and these ten toes upon my hands. May I help myself to wine? I thank you respectfully. By God's grace, you have a very superior vintage."

The lord of Brisetout walked to and fro with his hands behind his back. Perhaps he was not yet quite settled in his mind about the parallel between thieves and soldiers; perhaps Villon had interested him by some cross-thread of sympathy; perhaps his wits were simply muddled by so much unfamiliar reasoning; but whatever the cause, he somehow yearned to convert the young man to a better way of thinking, and could not make up his mind to drive him forth again into the street.

"There is something more than I can understand in this," he said at length. "Your mouth is full of subtleties, and the devil has led you very far astray; but the devil is only a very weak spirit before God's truth, and all his subtleties vanish at a word of true honour, like darkness at morning. Listen to me once more. I learned long ago that a gentleman should live chivalrously and lovingly to God and the king and his lady; and though I have seen many strange things done, I have still striven to command my ways upon that rule. It is not only written in all noble histories, but in every man's heart, if he will take care to read. You speak of food and wine, and I know very well that hunger is a difficult trial to endure; but you do not speak of other wants; you say nothing of honour, of faith to God and other men, of courtesy, of love without reproach. It may be that I am not very wise, - and yet I think I am, - but you seem to me like one who has lost his way and made a great error in life. You are attending to the little wants, and you have totally forgotten the great and only real ones, like a man who should be doctoring toothache on the judgment day. For such things as honour and love and faith are not only nobler than food and drink, but indeed I think we desire them more, and suffer more sharply for their absence. I speak to you as I think you will most easily understand me. Are you not, while careful to fill your belly, disregarding another appetite in your heart, which spoils the pleasure of your life and keeps you continually wretched?"

Villon was sensibly nettled under all this sermonising.

"You think I have no sense of honour!" he cried. "I'm poor enough, God knows! It's hard to see rich people with their gloves, and you blowing in your hands. An empty belly is a bitter thing, although you speak so lightly of it. If you had had as many as I, perhaps you would change your tune. Anyway, I'm a thief, - make the most of that, - but I'm not a devil from hell, God strike me dead! I would have you to know I've an honour of my own, as good as yours, though I don't prate about it all day long, as if it was a God's miracle to have any. It seems quite natural to me; I keep it in its box till it's wanted. Why, now, look you here, how long have I been in this room with you? Did you not tell me you were alone in the house? Look at your gold plate! You're strong, if you like, but you're old and unarmed, and I have my knife. What did I want but a jerk of the elbow and here would have been you with the cold steel in your bowels, and there would have been me, linking in the streets, with an armful of golden cups! Did you suppose I hadn't wit enough to see that? and I scorned the action. There are your damned goblets, as safe as in a church; there are you, with your heart ticking as good as new; and here am I, ready to go out again as poor as I came in, with my one white that you threw in my teeth! And you think I have no sense of honour - God strike me dead!"

The old man stretched out his right arm. "I will tell you what you are," he said. "You are a rogue, my man, an impudent and black-hearted rogue and vagabond. I have passed an hour with you. Oh, believe me, I feel myself disgraced! And you have eaten and drunk at my table. But now I am sick at your presence; the day has come, and the night-bird should be off to his roost. Will you go before, or after?"

"Which you please," returned the poet, rising. "I believe you to be strictly honourable." He thoughtfully emptied his cup. "I wish I could add you were intelligent," he went on, knocking on his head with his knuckles. "Age! age! the brains stiff and rheumatic."

The old man preceded him from a point of self-respect; Villon followed, whistling, with his thumbs in his girdle.

"God pity you," said the lord of Brisetout at the door.

"Good-bye, papa," returned Villon, with a yawn. "Many thanks for the cold mutton."

The door closed behind him. The dawn was breaking over the white roofs. A chill, uncomfortable morning ushered in the day. Villon stood and heartily stretched himself in the middle of the road.

"A very dull old gentleman," he thought. "I wonder what his goblets may be worth?"

A LEAF IN THE STORM

The Berceau de Dieu was a little village in the valley of the Seine. As a lark drops its nest among the grasses, so a few peasant people had dropped their little farms and cottages amid the great green woods on the winding river. It was a pretty place, with one steep, stony street, shady with poplars and with elms; quaint houses, about whose thatch a cloud of white and gray pigeons fluttered all day long; a little aged chapel with a conical red roof; and great barns covered with ivy and thick creepers, red and purple, and lichens that were yellow in the sun. All around it were the broad, flowering meadows, with the sleek cattle of Normandy fattening in them, and the sweet dim forests where the young men and maidens went on every holy day and feast-day in the summer-time to seek for wood-anemones, and lilies of the pools, and the wild campanula, and the fresh dog-rose, and all the boughs and grasses that made their house-doors like garden bowers, and seemed to take the cushat's note and the linnet's song into their little temple of God.

The Berceau de Dieu was very old indeed. Men said that the hamlet had been there in the day of the Virgin of Orleans; and a stone cross of the twelfth century still stood by the great pond of water at the bottom of the street under the chestnut-tree, where the villagers gathered to gossip at sunset when their work was done. It had no city near it, and no town nearer than four leagues. It was in the green care of a pastoral district, thickly wooded and intersected with orchards. Its produce of wheat and oats and cheese and fruit and eggs was more than sufficient for its simple prosperity. Its people were hardy, kindly, laborious, happy; living round the little gray chapel in amity and good-fellowship. Nothing troubled it. War and rumours of war, revolutions and counter-revolutions, empires and insurrections, military and political questions - these all were for it things unknown and unheard of, mighty winds that arose and blew and swept the lands around it, but never came near enough to harm it, lying there, as it did in its loneliness like any lark's nest. Even in the great days of the Revolution it had been quiet. It had had a lord whom it loved in the old castle on the hill at whose feet it nestled; it had never tried to harm him, and it had wept bitterly when he had fallen at Jemmapes, and left no heir, and the chateau had crumbled into ivy-hung ruins. The thunder-heats of that dread time had scarcely scorched it. It had seen a few of its best youth march away to the chant of the Marseillaise to fight on the plains of Champagne; and it had been visited by some patriots in bonnets rouges and soldiers in blue uniforms, who had given it tricoloured cockades and bade it wear them in the holy name of the Republic one and indivisible. But it had not known what these meant, and its harvests had been reaped without the sound of a shot in its fields or any gleam of steel by its innocent hearths; so that the terrors and the tidings of those noble and ghastly years had left no impress on its generations.

Reine Allix, indeed, the oldest woman among them all, numbering more than ninety years, remembered when she was a child hearing her father and his neighbours talk in low, awe-stricken tones one bitter wintry night of how a king had been slain to save the people; and she remembered likewise - remembered it well, because it had been her betrothal night and the sixteenth birthday of her life - how a horseman had flashed through the startled street like a comet, and had called aloud, in a voice of fire, "Gloire! gloire! gloire! - Marengo! Marengo! Marengo!" and how the village had dimly understood that something marvellous for France had happened afar off, and how her brothers and her cousins and her betrothed, and she with them, had all gone up to the high slope over the river, and had piled up a great pyramid of pine wood and straw and dried mosses, and had set flame to it, till it had glowed in its scarlet triumph all through that wondrous night of the sultry summer of victory.

These and the like memories she would sometimes relate to the children at evening when they gathered round her begging for a story. Otherwise, no memories of the Revolution or the Empire disturbed the tranquility of the Berceau; and even she, after she had told them, would add, "I am not sure now what Marengo was. A battle, no doubt, but I am not sure where nor why. But we heard later that little Claudis, my aunt's youngest-born, a volunteer not nineteen, died at it. If we had known, we should not have gone up and lit the bonfire."

This woman, who had been born in that time of famine and flame, was the happiest creature in the whole hamlet of the Berceau. "I am old; yes, I am very old," she would say, looking up from her spinning-wheel in her house-door, and shading her eyes from the sun, "very old - ninety-two last summer. But when one has a roof over one's head, and a pot of soup always, and a grandson like mine, and when onc has lived all one's life in the Berceau de Dieu, then it is well to be so old. Ah, yes, my little ones, - yes, though you doubt it, you little birds that have just tried your wings, - it is well to be so old. One has time to think, and thank the good God, which one never seemed to have a minute to do in that work, work, work when one was young."

Reine Allix was a tall and strong woman, very withered and very bent and very brown, yet with sweet, dark, flashing eyes that had still light in them, and a face that was still noble, though nearly a century had bronzed it with its harvest suns and blown on it with its winter winds. She wore always the same garb of homely dark-blue serge, always the same tall white head-gear, always the same pure silver ear-rings that had been at once an heirloom and a nuptial gift. She was always shod in her wooden sabots, and she always walked abroad with a staff of ash. She had been born in the Berceau de Dieu; had lived there and wedded there; had toiled there all her life, and never left it for a greater distance than a league, or for a longer time than a day. She loved it with an intense love. The world beyond it was nothing to her; she scarcely believed in it as existing. She could neither read nor write. She told the truth, reared her offspring in honesty, and praised God always - had praised Him when starving in a bitter winter after her husband's death, when there had been no field work, and she had had five children to feed and clothe; and praised Him now that her sons were all dead before her, and all she had living of her blood was her grandson Bernadou.

Her life had been a hard one. Her parents had been hideously poor. Her marriage had scarcely bettered her condition. She had laboured in the fields always, hoeing and weeding and reaping and carrying wood and driving mules, and continually rising with the first streak of daybreak. She had known fever and famine and all manner of earthly ills. But now in her old age she had peace. Two of her dead sons, who had sought their fortunes in the other hemisphere, had left her a little money, and she had a little cottage and a plot of ground, and a pig, and a small orchard. She was well-to-do, and could leave it all to Bernadou; and for ten years she had been happy, perfectly happy, in the coolness and the sweetness and the old familiar ways and habits of the Berceau.

Bernadou was very good to her. The lad, as she called him, was five and twenty years old, tall and straight and clean-limbed, with the blue eyes of the North, and a gentle, frank face. He worked early and late in the plot of ground that gave him his livelihood. He lived with his grandmother, and tended her with a gracious courtesy and veneration that never altered. He was not very wise; he also could neither read nor write; he believed in his priest and his homestead, and loved the ground that he had trodden ever since his first steps from the cradle had been guided by Reine Allix. He had never been drawn for the conscription, because he was the only support of a woman of ninety; he likewise had never been half a dozen kilometres from his birthplace. When he was bidden to vote, and he asked what his vote of assent would pledge him to do, they told him, "It will bind you to honour your grandmother so long as she shall live, and to get up with the lark, and to go to mass every Sunday, and to be a loyal son to your country. Nothing more." And thereat he had smiled and straightened his stalwart frame, and gone right willingly to the voting-urn.

He was very stupid in these things; and Reine Allix,

though clear-headed and shrewd, was hardly more learned in them than he.

"Look you," she had said to him oftentimes, "in my babyhood there was the old white flag upon the chateau. Well, they pulled that down and put up a red one. That toppled and fell, and there was one of three colours. Then somebody with a knot of white lilies in his hand came one day and set up the old white one afresh; and before the day was done that was down again and the tricolour again up where it is. Now, some I know fretted themselves greatly because of all these changes of the flags; but as for me, I could not see that any one of them mattered: bread was just as dear and sleep was just as sweet whichever of the three was uppermost."

Bernadou, who had never known but the flag of three colours, believed her, as indeed he believed every word that those kindly and resolute old lips ever uttered to him.

He had never been in a city, and only once, on the day of his first communion, in the town four leagues away. He knew nothing more than this simple, cleanly, honest life that he led. With what men did outside his little world of meadow-land and woodland he had no care nor any concern. Once a man had come through the village of the Berceau, a travelling hawker of cheap prints, - a man with a wild eye and a restless brain, - who told Bernadou that he was a downtrodden slave, a clod, a beast like a mule, who fetched and carried that the rich might fatten, a dolt, an idiot, who cared nothing for the rights of man and the wrongs of the poor. Bernadou had listened with a perplexed face; then with a smile, that had cleared it like sunlight, he had answered, in his country dialect, "I do not know of what you speak. Rights? Wrongs? I cannot tell, But I have never owned a sou; I have never told a lie; I am strong enough to hold my own with any man that flouts me; and I am content where I am. That is enough for me."

The peddler had called him a poor-spirited beast of burden, but had said so out of reach of his arm, and by night had slunk away from the Berceau de Dieu, and had been no more seen there to vex the quiet contentment of its peaceful and peace-loving ways.

At night, indeed, sometimes, the little wine-shop of the village would be frequented by some half-dozen of the peasant proprietors of the place, who talked communism after their manner, not a very clear one, in excited tones and with the feverish glances of conspirators. But it meant little, and came to less. The weather and the price of wheat were dearer matters to them; and in the end they usually drank their red wine in amity, and went up the village street arm in arm, singing patriotic songs until their angry wives flung open their lattices and thrust their white head-gear out into the moonlight, and called to them shrewishly to get to bed and not make fools of themselves in that fashion; which usually silenced and sobered them all instantly; so that the revolutions of the Berceau de Dieu, if not quenched in a wine-pot, were always smothered in a nightcap, and never by any chance disturbed its repose.

But of these noisy patriots Bernadou was never one. He had the instinctive conservatism of the French peasant, which is in such direct and tough antagonism with the feverish socialism of the French artisan. His love was for the soil - a love deep-rooted as the oaks that grew in it. Of Paris he had a dim, vague dread, as of a superb beast continually draining and devouring. Of all forms of government he was alike ignorant. So long as he tilled his little angle of land in peace, so long as the sun ripened his fruits and corn, so long as famine was away from his door and his neighbours dwelt in good-fellowship with him, so long he was happy, and cared not whether he was thus happy under a monarchy, an empire, or a republic. This wisdom, which the peddler called apathy and cursed, the young man had imbibed from nature and the teachings of Reine Allix. "Look at home and mind thy word," she had said always to him. "It is labour enough for a man to keep his own life clean and his own hands honest. Be not thou at any time as they are who are for ever telling the good God how He might have made the world on a better plan, while the rats gnaw at their hay-stacks and the children cry over an empty platter."

And he had taken heed to her words, so that in all the country-side there was not any lad truer, gentler, braver, or more patient at labour than was Bernadou; and though some thought him mild even to foolishness, and meek even to stupidity, he was no fool; and he had a certain rough skill at music, and a rare gift at the culture of plants, and made his little home bright within the winter-time with melody, and in the summer gay without as a king's parterre.

At any rate, Reine Allix and he had been happy together for a quarter of a century under the old gray thatch of the wayside cottage, where it stood at the foot of the village street, with its great sycamores spread above it. Nor were they less happy when in mid-April, in the six and twentieth year of his age, Bernadou had come in with a bunch of primroses in his hand, and had bent down to her and saluted her with a respectful tenderness, and said softly and a little shyly, "Gran'mere, would it suit you if I were ever - to marry?"

Reine Allix was silent a minute and more, cherishing the primroses and placing them in a little brown cupful of water. Then she looked at him steadily with her clear, dark eyes. "Who is it, my child?" He was always a child to her, this last-born of the numerous brood that had once dwelt with her under the spreading branches of the sycamores, and had now all perished off the face of the earth, leaving himself and her alone.

Bernadou's eyes met hers frankly. "It is Margot Dal. Does that please you, gran'mere, or no?"

"It pleases me well," she said, simply. But there was a little quiver about her firm-set mouth, and her aged head was bent over the primroses. She had foreseen it; she was glad of it; and yet for the instant it was a pang to her.

"I am very thankful," said Bernadou, with a flash of joy on his face. He was independent of his grandmother; he could make enough to marry upon by his daily toil, and he had a little store of gold and silver in his bank in the thatch, put by for a rainy day; but he would have no more thought of going against her will than he would have thought of lifting his hand against her. In the primitive homesteads of the Berceau de Dieu filial reverence was still accounted the first of virtues, yet the simplest and the most imperative.

"I will go see Margot this evening," said Reine Allix, after a little pause. "She is a good girl and a brave, and of pure heart and fair name. You have chosen well, my grandson."

Bernadou stooped his tall, fair, curly head, and she laid her hands on him and blessed him.

That evening, as the sun set, Reine Allix kept her word, and went to the young maiden who had allured the eyes and heart of Bernadou. Margot was an orphan; she had not a penny to her dower; she had been brought up on charity, and she dwelt now in the family of the largest landowner of the place, a miller with numerous offspring, and several head of cattle, and many stretches of pasture and of orchard. Margot worked for a hard master, living indeed as one of the family, but sharply driven all day long at all manner of housework and field work. Reine Allix had kept her glance on her, through some instinctive sense of the way that Bernadou's thoughts were turning, and she had seen much to praise, nothing to chide, in the young girl's modest, industrious, cheerful, uncomplaining life. Margot was very pretty, too, with the brown oval face and the great black soft eyes and the beautiful form of the Southern blood that had run in the veins of her father, who had been a sailor of Marseilles, while her mother had been a native of the Provencal country. Altogether, Reine Allix knew that her beloved one could not have done better or more wisely, if choose at all he must. "Some people, indeed," she said to herself as she climbed the street whose sharp-set flints had been trodden by her wooden shoes for ninety years - "Some people would mourn and scold because there is no store of linen, no piece of silver plate, no little round sum in money with the poor child. But what does it matter? We have enough for three. It is wicked indeed for parents to live so that they leave their daughter portionless, but it is no fault of the child's. Let them say what they like, it is a reason the more that she should want a roof over her head and a husband to care for her good."

So she climbed the steep way and the slanting road round the hill, and went in by the door of the mill-house, and found Margot busy in washing some spring lettuces and other green things in a bowl of bright water. Reine Allix, in the fashion of her country and her breeding, was about to confer with the master and mistress ere saying a word to the girl, but there was that in Margot's face and in her timid greeting that lured speech out of her. She looked long and keenly into the child's downcast countenance, then touched her with a tender smile. "Petite Margot, the birds told me a little secret to-day. Canst guess what it is? Say?"

Margot coloured and then grew pale. True, Bernadou had never really spoken to her, but still, when one is seventeen, and has danced a few times with the same person, and has plucked the leaves of a daisy away to learn one's fortune, spoken words are not very much wanted.

At sight of her the eyes of the old woman moistened and grew dimmer than age had made them; she smiled still, but the smile had the sweetness of a blessing in it, and no longer the kindly banter of humour. "You love him, my little one?" she said, in a soft, hushed voice.

"Ah, madame!" Margot could not say more. She covered her face with her hands, and turned to the wall, and wept with a passion of joy.

Down in the Berceau there were gossips who would

have said, with wise shakes of their heads, "Tut, tut! how easy it is to make believe in a little love when one is a serving-maid, and has not a sou, nor a roof, nor a friend in the world, and a comely youth well-to-do is willing to marry us!"

But Reine Allix knew better. She had not lived ninety years in the world not to be able to discern between true feeling and counterfeit. She was touched, and drew the trembling frame of Margot into her arms, and kissed her twice on the closed, blue-veined lids of her black eyes. "Make him happy, only make him happy," she murmured; "for I am very old, Margot, and he is alone, all alone."

And the child crept to her, sobbing for very rapture that she, friendless, homeless, and penniless, should be thus elected for so fair a fate, and whispered through her tears, "I will."

Reine Allix spoke in all form to the miller and his wife, and with as much earnestness in her demand as though she had been seeking the hand of rich Yacobe, the tavern-keeper's only daughter. The people assented; they had no pretext to oppose; and Reine Allix wrapped her cloak about her and descended the hill and the street just as the twilight closed in and the little lights began to glimmer through the lattices and the shutters and the green mantle of the boughs, while the red fires of the smithy forge glowed brightly in the gloom, and a white horse waited to be shod, a boy in a blue blouse seated on its back and switching away with a branch of budding hazel the first gray gnats of the early year.

"It is well done, it is well done," she said to herself,

looking at the low rosy clouds and the pale gold of the waning sky. "A year or two, and I shall be in my grave. I shall leave him easier if I know he has some creature to care for him, and I shall be quiet in my coffin, knowing that his children's children will live on and on and on in the Berceau, and sometimes perhaps think a little of me when the nights are long and they sit round the fire."

She went in out of the dewy air, into the little low, square room of her cottage, and went up to Bernadou and laid her hands on his shoulders.

"Be it well with thee, my grandson, and with thy sons' sons after thee," she said solemnly. "Margot will be thy wife. May thy days and hers be long in thy birthplace!"

A month later they were married. It was then May. The green nest of the Berceau seemed to overflow with the singing of birds and the blossoming of flowers. The corn-lands promised a rare harvest, and the apple orchards were weighed down with their red and white blossoms. The little brown streams in the woods brimmed over in the grass, and the air was full of sweet mellow sunlight, a cool fragrant breeze, a continual music of humming bees and soaring larks and mule-bells ringing on the roads, and childish laughter echoing from the fields.

In this glad springtime Bernadou and Margot were wedded, going with their friends one sunny morning up the winding hill-path to the little gray chapel whose walls were hidden in ivy, and whose sorrowful Christ looked down through the open porch across the blue and hazy width of the river. Georges, the baker, whose fiddle made merry melody at all the village dances, played before them tunefully; little children, with their hands full of wood-flowers, ran before them; his old blind poodle smelt its way faithfully by their footsteps; their priest led the way upward with the cross held erect against the light; Reine Allix walked beside them, nearly as firmly as she had trodden the same road seventy years before in her own bridal hour. In the hollow below lay the Berceau de Dieu, with its red gables and its thatched roofs hidden beneath leaves, and its peaceful pastures smiling under the serene blue skies of France.

They were happy - ah, heaven, so happy! - and all their little world rejoiced with them.

They came home and their neighbours entered with them, and ate and drank, and gave them good wishes and gay songs, and the old priest blessed them with a father's tenderness upon their threshold; and the fiddle of Georges sent gladdest dance-music flying through the open casements, across the road, up the hill, far away to the clouds and the river.

At night, when the guests had departed and all was quite still within and without, Reine Allix sat alone at her window in the roof, thinking of their future and of her past, and watching the stars come out, one by another, above the woods. From her lattice in the eaves she saw straight up the village street; saw the dwellings of her lifelong neighbours, the slopes of the rich fields, the gleam of the broad gray water, the whiteness of the crucifix against the darkened skies. She saw it all - all so familiar, with that intimate association only possible to the peasant who has dwelt on one spot from birth to age. In that faint light, in those deep shadows, she could trace all the scene as though the brightness of the moon shone on it; it was all, in its homeliness and simplicity, intensely dear to her. In the playtime of her childhood, in the courtship of her youth, in the joys and woes of her wifehood and widowhood, the bitter pains and sweet ecstasies of her maternity, the hunger and privation of struggling desolate years, the contentment and serenity of old age - in all these her eyes had rested only on this small, quaint, leafy street, with its dwellings close and low, like bee-hives in a garden, and its pasture-lands and corn-lands, wood-girt and water-fed, stretching as far as the sight could reach. Every inch of its soil, every turn of its paths, was hallowed to her with innumerable memories; all her beloved dead were garnered there where the white Christ watched them; when her time should come, she thought, she would rest with them nothing loath. As she looked, the tears of thanksgiving rolled down her withered cheeks, and she bent herfeeble limbs and knelt down in the moonlight, praising God that He had given her to live and die in this cherished home, and beseeching Him for her children that they likewise might dwell in honesty, and with length of days abide beneath that roof.

"God is good," she murmured, as she stretched herself to sleep beneath the eaves, - "God is good. Maybe, when He takes me to Himself, if I be worthy, He will tell His holy saints to give me a little corner in His kingdom, that He shall fashion for me in the likeness of the Berceau." For it seemed to her that, than the Berceau, heaven itself could hold no sweeter or fairer nook of Paradise.

The year rolled on, and the cottage under the sycamores was but the happier for its new inmate. Bernadou was serious of temper, though so gentle, and the arch, gay humour of his young wife was like perpetual sunlight in the house. Margot, too, was so docile, so eager, so bright, and so imbued with devotional reverence for her husband and his home, that Reine Allix day by day blessed the fate that had brought to her this fatherless and penniless child. Bernadou himself spoke little; words were not in his way; but his blue, frank eyes shone with an unclouded radiance that never changed, and his voice, when he did speak, had a mellow softness in it that made his slightest speech to the two women with him tender as a caress.

"Thou art a happy woman, my sister," said the priest, who was well-nigh as old as herself.

Reine Allix bowed her head and made the sign of the cross. "I am, praise be to God!"

And being happy, she went to the hovel of poor Madelon Dreux, the cobbler's widow, and nursed her and her children through a malignant fever, sitting early and late, and leaving her own peaceful hearth for the desolate hut with the delirious ravings and heartrending moans of the fever-stricken. "How ought one to dare to be happy if one is not of use?" she would say to those who sought to dissuade her from running such peril.

Madelon Dreux and her family recovered, owing to her their lives; and she was happier than before, thinking of them when she sat on the settle before the wood fire roasting chestnuts and spinning flax on the wheel, and ever and again watching the flame reflected on the fair head of Bernadou or in the dark, smiling eyes of Margot.

Another spring passed and another year went by, and the little home under the sycamores was still no less honest in its labours or bright in its rest. It was one among a million of such homes in France, where a sunny temper made mirth with a meal of herbs, and filial love touched to poetry the prose of daily household tasks.

A child was born to Margot in the springtime with the violets and daisies, and Reine Allix was proud of the fourth generation, and, as she caressed the boy's healthy, fair limbs, thought that God was indeed good to her, and that her race would live long in the place of her birth. The child resembled Bernadou, and had his clear, candid eyes. It soon learned to know the voice of "gran'mere," and would turn from its young mother's bosom to stretch its arms to Reine Allix. It grew fair and strong, and all the ensuing winter passed its hours curled like a dormouse or playing like a puppy at her feet in the chimney-corner. Another spring and summer came, and the boy was more than a year old, with curls of gold, and cheeks like apples, and a mouth that always smiled. He could talk a little, and tumbled like a young rabbit among the flowering grasses. Reine Allix watched him, and her eyes filled. "God is too good," she thought. She feared that she should scarce be so willing to go to her last sleep under the trees on the hillside as she used to be. She could not help a desire to see this child, this second Bernadou, grow up to youth and manhood; and of this she knew it was wild to dream.

It was ripe midsummer. The fields were all russet and amber with an abundance of corn. The little gardens had seldom yielded so rich a produce. The cattle and the flocks were in excellent health. There had never been a season of greater promise and prosperity for the little traffic that the village and its farms drove in sending milk and sheep and vegetable wealth to that great city which was to it as a dim, wonderful, mystic name without meaning.

One evening in this gracious and golden time the people sat out as usual when the day was done, talking from door to door, the old women knitting or spinning, the younger ones mending their husbands' or brothers' blouses or the little blue shirts of their infants, the children playing with the dogs on the sward that edged the stones of the street, and above all the great calm heavens and the glow of the sun that had set.

Reine Allix, like the others, sat before the door, for once doing nothing, but with folded hands and bended head dreamily taking pleasure in the coolness that had come with evening, and the smell of the limes that were in blossom, and the blithe chatter of Margot with the neighbours. Bernadou was close beside them, watering and weeding those flowers that were at once his pride and his recreation, making the face of his dwelling bright and the air around it full of fragrance.

The little street was quiet in the evening light, only the laughter of the children and the gay gossip of their mothers breaking the pleasant stillness; it had been thus at evening with the Berceau centuries before their time; they thought that it would thus likewise be when the centuries should have seen the youngest-born there in his grave.

Suddenly came along the road between the trees an old man and a mule; it was Mathurin, the miller, who had been that day to a little town four leagues off, which was the trade-mart and the corn-exchange of the district. He paused before the cottage of Reine Allix; he was dusty, travel-stained, and sad. Margot ceased laughing among her flowers as she saw her old master. None of them knew why, yet the sight of him made the air seem cold and the night seem near.

"There is terrible news," he said, drawing a sheet of printed words from his coat-pocket - "terrible news! We are to go to war."

"War!" The whole village clustered round him. They had heard of war, far-off wars in Africa and Mexico, and some of their sons had been taken off like young wheat mown before its time; but it still remained to them a thing remote, impersonal, inconceivable, with which they had nothing to do, nor ever would have anything.

"Read!" said the old man, stretching out his sheet. The only one there who could do so, Picot, the tailor, took it and spelled the news out to their wondering ears. It was the declaration of France against Prussia.

There arose a great wail from the mothers whose sons were conscripts. The rest asked in trembling, "Will it touch us?"

"Us!" echoed Picot, the tailor, in contempt. "How should it touch us? Our braves will be in Berlin with another fortnight. The paper says so."

The people were silent; they were not sure what he meant by Berlin, and they were afraid to ask.

"My boy! My boy!" wailed one woman, smiting her

breast. Her son was in the army.

"Marengo!" murmured Reine Allix, thinking of that far-off time in her dim youth when the horseman had flown through the dusky street and the bonfire had blazed on the highest hill above the river.

"Bread will be dear," muttered Mathurin, the miller, going onward with his foot-weary mule. Bernadou stood silent, with his roses dry and thirsty round him.

"Why art thou sad?" whispered Margot, with wistful eyes. "Thou art exempt from war service, my love?"

Bernadou shook his head. "The poor will suffer somehow," was all he answered.

Yet to him, as to all the Berceau, the news was not very terrible, because it was so vague and distant - an evil so far off and shapeless.

Monsieur Picot, the tailor, who alone could read, ran from house to house, from group to group, breathless, gay, and triumphant, telling them all that in two weeks more their brethren would sup in the king's palace at Berlin; and the people believed and laughed and chattered, and, standing outside their doors in the cool nights, thought that some good had come to them and theirs.

Only Reine Allix looked up to the hill above the river and murmured, "When we lit the bonfire there, Claudis lay dead;" and Bernadou, standing musing among his roses, said, with a smile that was very grave, "Margot, see here! When Picot shouted, 'A Berlin!' he trod on my Gloire de Dijon rose and killed it."

The sultry heats and cloudless nights of the wondrous and awful summer of the year 1870 passed by, and to the Berceau de Dieu it was a summer of fair promise and noble harvest, and never had the land brought forth in richer profusion for man and beast. Some of the youngest and ablest-bodied labourers were indeed drawn away to join those swift trains that hurried thousands and tens of thousands to the frontier by the Rhine. But most of the male population were married, and were the fathers of young children; and the village was only moved to a thrill of love and of honest pride to think how its young Louis and Jean and Andre and Valentin were gone full of high hope and high spirit, to come back, maybe, - who could say not? - with epaulets and ribbons of honour. Why they were gone they knew not very clearly, but their superiors affirmed that they were gone to make greater the greatness of France; and the folk of the Berceau believed it, having in a corner of their quiet hearts a certain vague, dormant, yet deep-rooted love, on which was written the name of their country.

News came slowly and seldom to the Berceau. Unless some one of the men rode his mule to the little town, which was but very rarely, or unless some peddler came through the village with a news-sheet or so in his pack or rumours and tidings on his lips, nothing that was done beyond its fields and woods came to it. And the truth of what it heard it had no means of measuring or sifting. It believed what it was told, without questioning; and as it reaped the harvests in the rich hot sun of August, its peasants laboured cheerily in the simple and firm belief that mighty things were being done for them and theirs in the far eastern provinces by their great army, and that Louis and Jean and Andre and Valentin and the rest - though indeed no tidings had been heard of them - were safe and well and glorious somewhere, away where the sun rose, in the sacked palaces of the German king. Reine Allix alone of them was serious and sorrowful, she whose memories stretched back over the wide space of near a century.

"Why art thou anxious, gran'mere?" they said to her. "There is no cause. Our army is victorious everywhere; and they say our lads will send us all the Prussians' corn and cattle, so that the very beggars will have their stomachs full."

But Reine Allix shook her head, sitting knitting in the sun. "My children, I remember the days of my youth. Our army was victorious then; at least, they said so. Well, all I know is that little Claudis and the boys with him never came back; and as for bread, you could not get it for love or money, and the people lay dead of famine out on the public roads."

"But that is so long ago, gran'mere!" they urged.

Reine Allix nodded. "Yes, it is long ago, my dears. But I do not think that things change very much."

They were silent out of respect for her, but among themselves they said, "She is very old. Nothing is as it was in her time."

One evening, when the sun was setting red over the reapen fields, two riders on trembling and sinking horses went through the village using whip and spur, and scarcely drew rein as they shouted to the cottagers to know whether they had seen go by a man running for his life. The people replied that they had seen nothing of the kind, and the horsemen pressed on, jamming their spurs into their poor beasts' steaming flanks. "If you see him, catch and hang him," they shouted, as they scoured away; "he is a Prussian spy!"

"A Prussian!" the villagers echoed, with a stupid stare - "a Prussian in France!"

One of the riders looked over his shoulder for a moment. "You fools! Do you not know? We are beaten, - beaten everywhere, - and the Prussian pigs march on Paris."

The spy was not seen in the Berceau, but the news brought by his pursuers scared sleep from the eyes of every grown man that night in the little village. "It is the accursed Empire!" screamed the patriots of the wine-shop. But the rest of the people were too terrified and down-stricken to take heed of empires or patriots; they only thought of Louis and Jean and Andre and Valentin; and they collected round Reine Allix, who said to them, "My children, for love of money all our fairest fruits and flowers - yea, even to the best blossoms of our maidenhood - were sent to be bought and sold in Paris. We sinned therein, and this is the will of God."

This was all for a time that they heard. It was a place lowly and obscure enough to be left in peace. The law pounced down on it once or twice and carried off a few more of its men for army service, and arms were sent to it from its neighbouring town, and an old soldier of the First Empire tried to instruct its remaining sons in their use. But he had no apt pupil except Bernadou, who soon learned to handle a musket with skill and with precision, and who carried his straight form gallantly and well, though his words were seldom heard and his eyes were always sad.

"You will not be called till the last, Bernadou," said the old soldier; "you are married, and maintain your grandam and wife and child. But a strong, muscular, well-built youth like you should not wait to be called; you should volunteer to serve France."

"I will serve France when my time comes," said Bernadou, simply, in answer. But he would not leave his fields barren, and his orchard uncared for, and his wife to sicken and starve, and his grandmother to perish alone in her ninety-third year. They jeered and flouted and upbraided him, those patriots who screamed against the fallen Empire in the wine-shop; but he looked them straight in the eyes, and held his peace, and did his daily work.

"If he is called, he will not be found wanting," said Reine Allix, who knew him better than did even the young wife whom he loved.

Bernadou clung to his home with a dogged devotion. He would not go from it to fight unless compelled, but for it he would have fought like a lion. His love for his country was only an indefinite, shadowy existence that was not clear to him; he could not save a land that he had never seen, a capital that was only to him as an empty name; nor could he comprehend the danger that his nation ran, nor could he desire to go forth and spend his life-blood in defence of things unknown to him. He was only a peasant, and he could not read nor greatly understand. But affection for his birthplace was a passion with him, mute indeed, but deep-seated as an oak. For his birthplace he would have struggled as a man can only struggle when supreme love as well as duty nerves his arm. Neither he nor Reine Allix could see that a man's duty might lie from home, but in that home both were alike ready to dare anything and to suffer everything. It was a narrow form of patriotism, yet it had nobleness, endurance, and patience in it; in song it has been oftentimes deified as heroism, but in modern warfare it is punished as the blackest crime.

So Bernadou tarried in his cottage till he should be called, keeping watch by night over the safety of his village, and by day doing all he could to aid the deserted wives and mothers of the place by the tilling of their ground for them and the tending of such poor cattle as were left in their desolate fields. He and Margot and Reine Allix, between them, fed many mouths that would otherwise have been closed in death by famine, and denied themselves all except the barest and most meagre subsistence, that they might give away the little they possessed.

And all this while the war went on, but seemed far from them, so seldom did any tidings of it pierce the seclusion in which they dwelt. By-and-by, as the autumn went on, they learned a little more. Fugitives coming to the smithy for a horse's shoe; women fleeing to their old village homes from their base, gay life in the city; mandates from thegovernment of defence sent to every hamlet in the country; stray news-sheets brought in by carriers or hawkers and hucksters - all these by degrees told them of the peril of their country, vaguely indeed, and seldom truthfully, but so that by mutilated rumours they came at last to know the awful facts of the fate of Sedan, the fall of the Empire, the siege of Paris. It did not alter their daily lives; it was still too far off and too impalpable. But a foreboding, a dread, an unspeakable woe settled down on them. Already their lands and cattle had been harassed to yield provision for the army and large towns; already their best horses had been taken for the siege-trains and the forage-waggons; already their ploughshares were perforce idle, and their children cried because of the scarcity of nourishment; already the iron of war had entered their souls.

The little street at evening was mournful and very silent; the few who talked spoke in whispers, lest a spy should hear them, and the young ones had no strength to play - they wanted food.

"It is as it was in my youth," said Reine Allix, eating her piece of black bread and putting aside the better food prepared for her, that she might save it, unseen, for the "child."

It was horrible to her and to all of them to live in that continual terror of an unknown foe, that perpetual expectation of some ghastly, shapeless misery. They were quiet, - so quiet! - but by all they heard they knew that any night, as they went to their beds, the thunder of cannon might awaken them; any morning, as they looked on their beloved fields, they knew that ere sunset the flames of war might have devoured them. They knew so little too; all they were told was so indefinite and garbled that sometimes they thought the whole was some horrid dream - thought so, at least, until they looked at their empty stables, their untilled land, their children who cried from hunger, their mothers who wept for the conscripts.

But as yet it was not so very much worse than it had been in times of bad harvest and of dire distress; and the storm which raged over the land had as yet spared this little green nest among the woods on the Seine.

November came. "It is a cold night, Bernadou; put on some more wood," said Reine Allix. Fuel at the least was plentiful in that district, and Bernadou obeyed.

He sat at the table, working at a new churn for his wife; he had some skill at turnery and at invention in such matters. The child slept soundly in its cradle by the hearth, smiling while it dreamed. Margot spun at her wheel. Reine Allix sat by the fire, seldom lifting her head from her long knitting-needles, except to cast a look on her grandson or at the sleeping child. The little wooden shutter of the house was closed. Some winter roses bloomed in a pot beneath the little crucifix. Bernadou's flute lay on a shelf; he had not had heart enough to play it since the news of the war had come.

Suddenly a great sobbing cry rose without - the cry of many voices, all raised in woe together. Bernadou rose, took his musket in his hand, undid his door, and looked out. All the people were turned out into the street, and the women, loudly lamenting, beat their breasts and strained their children to their bosoms. There was a sullen red light in the sky to the eastward, and on the wind a low, hollow roar stole to them.

"What is it?" he asked.

"The Prussians are on us!" answered twenty voices in one accord. "That red glare is the town burning."

Then they were all still - a stillness that was more horrible than their lamentations. Reinc Allix came and stood by her grandson. "If we must die, let us die here," she said, in a voice that was low and soft and grave.

He took her hand and kissed it. She was content with his answer.

Margot stole forth too, and crouched behind them, holding her child to her breast. "What can they do to us?" she asked, trembling, with the rich colours of her face blanched white.

Bernadou smiled on her. "I do not know, my dear. I think even they can hardly bring death upon women and children."

"They can, and they will," said a voice from the crowd.

None answered. The street was very quiet in the darkness. Far away in the east the red glare glowed. On the wind was still that faint, distant, ravening roar, like the roar of famished wolves; it was the roar of fire and of war.

In the silence Reine Allix spoke: "God is good. Shall we not trust in Him?"

With one great choking sob the people answered; their hearts were breaking. All night long they watched in the street - they who had done no more to bring this curse upon them than the flower-roots that slept beneath the snow. They dared not go to their beds; they knew not when the enemy might be upon them. They dared not flee; even in their own woods the foe might lurk for them. One man indeed did cry aloud, "Shall we stay here in our houses to be smoked out like bees from their hives? Let us fly!"

But the calm, firm voice of Reine Allix rebuked him: "Let who will, run like a hare from the hounds. For me and mine, we abide by our homestead."

And they were ashamed to be outdone by a woman, and a woman of ninety years old, and no man spoke any more of flight. All the night long they watched in the cold and the wind, the children shivering beneath their mothers' skirts, the men sullenly watching the light of the flames in the dark, starless sky. All night long they were left alone, though far off they heard the dropping shots of scattered firing, and in the leafless woods around them the swift flight of woodland beasts startled from their sleep, and the hurrying feet of sheep terrified from their folds in the outlying fields.

The daybreak came, gray, cheerless, very cold. A dense fog, white and raw, hung over the river; in the east, where the sun, they knew, was rising, they could only see the livid light of the still towering flames and pillars of black smoke against the leaden clouds.

"We will let them come and go in peace if they will," murmured old Mathurin. "What can we do? We have no arms, no powder hardly, no soldiers, no defence."

Bernadou said nothing, but he straightened his tall limbs, and in his grave blue eyes a light gleamed.

Reine Allix looked at him as she sat in the doorway of her house. "Thy hands are honest, thy heart pure, thy conscience clear. Be not afraid to die if need there be," she said to him.

He looked down and smiled on her. Margot clung to him in a passion of weeping. He clasped her close and kissed her softly, but the woman who read his heart was the woman who had held him at his birth.

By degrees the women crept timidly back into their houses, hiding their eyes so that they should not see that horrid light against the sky, while the starving children clung to their breasts or to their skirts, wailing aloud in terror. The few men there were left, for the most part of them very old or else mere striplings, gathered together in a hurried council. Old Mathurin, the miller, and the patriots of the wine-shop were agreed that there should be no resistance, whatever might befall them; that it would be best to hide such weapons as they had and any provisions that still remained to them, and yield up themselves and their homes with humble grace to the dire foe. "If we do otherwise," they said, "the soldiers will surely slay us, and what can a miserable little hamlet like this achieve against cannon and steel and fire?"

Bernadou alone raised his voice in opposition. His eye kindled, his cheek flushed, his words for once sprang from his lips like fire. "What!" he said to them, "shall we yield up our homes and our wives and our infants without a single blow? Shall we be so vile as to truckle to the enemies of France and show that we can fear them? It were a shame, a foul shame; we were not worthy of the name of men. Let us prove to them that there are people in France who are not afraid to die. Let us hold our own so long as we can. Our muskets are good, our walls strong, our woods in this weather morasses that will suck in and swallow them if only we have tact to drive them there. Let us do what we can. The camp of the francs-tireurs is but three leagues form us. They will be certain to come to our aid. At any rate, let us die bravely. We can do little, that may be; but if every man in France does that little that he can, that little will be great enough to drive the invaders off the soil."

Mathurin and the others screamed at him and hooted. "You are a fool!" they shouted. "You will be the undoing of us all. Do you not know that one shot fired, nay, only one musket found, and the enemy puts a torch to the whole place?"

"I know," said Bernadou, with a dark radiance in his azure eyes. "But then it is a choice between disgrace and the flames; let us only take heed to be clear of the first - the last must rage as God wills."

But they screamed and mouthed and hissed at him: "Oh yes! fine talk, fine talk! See your own roof in flames if you will; you shall not ruin ours. Do what you will with your own neck; keep it erect or hang by it, as you choose. But you have no right to give your neighbours over to death, whether they will or no."

He strove, he pleaded, he conjured, he struggled with them half the night, with the salt tears running down his cheeks, and all his gentle blood burning with righteous wrath and loathing shame, stirred for the first time in all his life to a rude, simple, passionate eloquence. But they were not persuaded. Their few gold pieces hidden in the rafters, their few feeble sheep starving in the folds, their own miserable lives, all hungry, woe-begone, and spent in daily terrors - these were still dear to them, and they would not imperil them. They called him a madman; they denounced him as one who would be their murderer; they threw themselves on him and demanded his musket, to bury it with the rest under the altar in the old chapel on the hill.

Bernadou's eyes flashed fire; his breast heaved; his nerves quivered; he shook them off and strode a step forward. "As you live," he muttered, "I have a mind to fire on you, rather than let you live to shame yourselves and me!"

Reine Allix, who stood by him silent all the while, laid her hand on his shoulder. "My boy," she said in his ear, "you are right, and they are wrong. Yet let not dissension between brethren open the door for the enemy to enter thereby into your homes. Do what you will with your own life, Bernadou, - it is yours, - but leave them to do as they will with theirs. You cannot make sheep into lions, and let not the first blood shed here be a brother's."

Bernadou's head dropped on his breast. "Do as you will," he muttered to his neighbours. They took his musket from him, and in the darkness of the night stole silently up the wooded chapel hill and buried it, with all their other arms, under the altar where the white Christ hung. "We are safe now," said Mathurin, the miller, to the patriots of the tavern. "Had that madman had his way, he had destroyed us all."

Reine Allix softly led her grandson across his own threshold, and drew his head down to hers, and kissed him between the eyes. "You did what you could, Bernadou," she said to him; "let the rest come as it will."

Then she turned from him, and flung her cloak over

her head, and sank down, weeping bitterly; for she had lived through ninety-three years only to see this agony at the last.

Bernadou, now that all means of defence was gone from him, and the only thing left to him to deal with was his own life, had become quiet and silent and passionless, as was his habit. He would have fought like a mastiff for his home, but this they had forbidden him to do, and he was passive and without hope. He shut to his door, and sat down with his hand in that of Reine Allix and his arm around his wife. "There is nothing to do but to wait," he said, sadly. The day seemed very long in coming.

The firing ceased for a while; then its roll commenced afresh, and grew nearer to the village. Then again all was still.

At noon a shepherd staggered into the place, pale, bleeding, bruised, covered with mire. The Prussians, he told them, had forced him to be their guide, had knotted him tight to a trooper's saddle, and had dragged him with them until he was half dead with fatigue and pain. At night he had broken from them and had fled. They were close at hand, he said, and had burned the town from end to end because a man had fired at them from a housetop. That was all he knew. Bernadou, who had gone out to hear his news, returned into the house and sat down and hid his face within his hands. "If I resist you are all lost," he muttered. "And yet to yield like a cur!" It was a piteous question, whether to follow the instinct in him and see his birthplace in flames and his family slaughtered for his act, or to crush out the manhood in him and live, loathing himself as a coward for evermore.

Reine Allix looked at him, and laid her hand on his bowed head, and her voice was strong and tender as music: "Fret not thyself, my beloved. When the moment comes, then do as thine own heart and the whisper of God in it bid thee."

A great sob answered her; it was the first since his earliest infancy that she had ever heard from Bernadou.

It grew dark. The autumn day died. The sullen clouds dropped scattered rain. The red leaves were blown in millions by the wind. The little houses on either side the road were dark, for the dwellers in them dared not show any light that might be a star to allure to them the footsteps of their foes. Bernadou sat with his arms on the table, and his head resting on them. Margot nursed her son. Reine Allix prayed.

Suddenly in the street without there was the sound of many feet of horses and of men, the shouting of angry voices, the splashing of quick steps in the watery ways, the screams of women, the flash of steel through the gloom. Bernadou sprang to his feet, his face pale, his blue eyes dark as night. "They are come!" he said, under his breath. It was not fear that he felt, nor horror; it was rather a passion of love for his birthplace and his nation - a passion of longing to struggle and to die for both. And he had no weapon!

He drew his house-door open with a steady hand, and stood on his own threshold and faced these his enemies. The street was full of them, some mounted, some on foot; crowds of them swarmed in the woods and on the roads. They had settled on the village as vultures on a dead lamb's body. It was a little, lowly place; it might well have been left in peace. It had had no more share in the war than a child still unborn, but it came in the victors' way, and their mailed heel crushed it as they passed. They had heard that arms were hidden and francs-tireurs sheltered there, and they had swooped down on it and held it hard and fast. Some were told off to search the chapel; some to ransack the dwellings; some to seize such food and bring such cattle as there might be left; some to seek out the devious paths that crossed and recrossed the fields; and yet there remained in the little street hundreds of armed men, force enough to awe a citadel or storm a breach.

The people did not attempt to resist. They stood passive, dry-eyed in misery, looking on while the little treasures of their household lives were swept away for ever, and ignorant what fate by fire or iron might be their portion ere the night was done. They saw the corn that was their winter store to save their offspring from famine poured out like ditch-water. They saw oats and wheat flung down to be trodden into a slough of mud and filth. They saw the walnut presses in their kitchens broken open, and their old heirlooms of silver, centuries old, borne away as booty. They saw the oak cupboards in their wives' bed-chambers ransacked, and the homespun linen and the quaint bits of plate that had formed their nuptial dowers cast aside in derision or trampled into a battered heap. They saw the pet lamb of their infants, the silver ear-rings of their brides, the brave tankards they had drunk their marriage wine in, the tame bird that flew to their whistle, all seized for food or seized for spoil. They saw all this, and had to stand by with mute tongues and passive hands, lest any glance of wrath or gesture of revenge should bring the leaden bullet in their children's throats or the yellow flame amid their homesteads. Greater agony the world cannot hold.

Under the porch of the cottage, by the sycamores, one group stood and looked, silent and very still: Bernadou, erect, pale, calm, with a fierce scorn burning in his eyes; Margot, quiet because he wished her so, holding to her the rosy and golden beauty of her son; Reine Allix, with a patient horror on her face, her figure drawn to its full height, and her hands holding to her breast the crucifix. They stood thus, waiting they knew not what, only resolute to show no cowardice and meet no shame.

Behind them was the dull, waning glow of the wood fire on the hearth which had been the centre of all their hopes and joys; before them the dim, dark country, and the woe-stricken faces of their neighbours, and the moving soldiery with their torches, and the quivering forms of the half-dying horses.

Suddenly a voice arose from the armed mass: "Bring me the peasant hither."

Bernadou was seized by several hands and forced and dragged from his door out to the place where the leader of the uhlans sat on a white charger that shook and snorted blood in its exhaustion. Bernadou cast off the alien grasp that held him, and stood erect before his foes. He was no longer pale, and his eyes were clear and steadfast.

"You look less a fool than the rest," said the Prussian commander. "You know this country well?"

"Well!" The country in whose fields and woodlands he had wandered from his infancy, and whose every meadow-path and wayside tree and flower-sown brook he knew by heart as a lover knows the lines of his mistress's face!

"You have arms here?" pursued the German.

"We had."

"What have you done with them?"

"If I had had my way, you would not need ask. You would have felt them."

The Prussian looked at him keenly, doing homage to the boldness of the answer. "Will you confess where they are?"

"No."

"You know the penalty for concealment of arms is death?"

"You have made it so."

"We have, and Prussian will is French law. You are a bold man; you merit death. But still, you know the country well?"

Bernadou smiled, as a mother might smile were any foolish enough to ask her if she remembered the look her dead child's face had worn.

"If you know it well," pursued the Prussian, "I will give you a chance. Lay hold of my stirrup-leather and be lashed to it, and show me straight as the crow flies to where the weapons are hidden. If you do, I will leave you your life. If you do not - "

"If I do not?"

"You will be shot."

Bernadou was silent; his eyes glanced through the mass of soldiers to the little cottage under the trees opposite. The two there were straining to behold him, but the soldiers pushed them back, so that in the flare of the torches they could not see, nor in the tumult hear. He thanked God for it.

"Your choice?" asked the uhlan, impatiently, after a moment's pause.

Bernadou's lips were white, but they did not tremble as he answered, "I am no traitor." And his eyes, as he spoke, went softly to the little porch where the light glowed from that hearth beside which he would never again sit with the creatures he loved around him.

The German looked at him. "Is that a boast, or a fact?"

"I am no traitor," Bernadou answered, simply, once more.

The Prussian gave a sign to his troopers. There was the sharp report of a double shot, and Bernadou fell dead. One bullet had pierced his brain, the other was bedded in his lungs. The soldiers kicked aside the warm and quivering body. It was only a peasant killed!

With a shriek that rose above the roar of the wind, and cut like steel to every human heart that beat there, Reine Allix forced her way through the throng, and fell on her knees beside him, and caught him in her arms, and laid his head upon her breast, where he had used to sleep his softest sleep in infancy and childhood. "It is God's will! it is God's will!" she muttered; and then she laughed - a laugh so terrible that the blood of the boldest there ran cold.

Margot followed her and looked, and stood dry-eyed and silent; then flung herself and the child she carried in her arms beneath the hoof of the white charger. "End your work!" she shrieked to them. "You have killed him - kill us. Have you not mercy enough for that?"

The horse, terrified and snorting blood, plunged and trampled the ground; his fore foot struck the child's golden head and stamped its face out of all human likeness. Some peasants pulled Margot from the lashing hoofs; she was quite dead, though neither wound nor bruise was on her.

Reine Allix neither looked nor paused. With all her strength she had begun to drag the body of Bernadou across the threshold of his house. "He shall lie at home, he shall lie at home," she muttered. She would not believe that already he was dead. With all the force of her earliest womanhood she lifted him, and half drew, half bore him into the house that he had loved, and laid him down upon the hearth, and knelt by him, caressing him as though he were once more a child, and saying softly, "Hush!" - for her mind was gone, and she fancied that he only slept.

Without, the tumult of the soldiery increased. They found the arms hidden under the altar on the hill; they seized five peasants to slay them for the dire offence.

The men struggled, and would not go as the sheep to the shambles. They were shot down in the street, before the eyes of their children. Then the order was given to fire the place in punishment, and leave it to its fate. The torches were flung with a laugh on the dry thatched roofs; brands snatched from the house fires on the hearths were tossed among the dwelling-houses and the barns. The straw and timber flared alight like tow.

An old man, her nearest neighbour, rushed to the cottage of Reine Allix and seized her by the arm. "They fire the Berceau," he screamed. "Quick! quick! or you will be burned alive!"

Reine Allix looked up with a smile. "Be quiet! Do you not see! He sleeps."

The old man shook her, implored her, strove to drag her away; in desperation pointed to the roof above, which was already in flames.

Reine Allix looked. At that sight her mind cleared, and regained consciousness; she remembered all, she understood all; she knew that he was dead. "Go in peace and save yourself," she said, in the old, sweet, strong tone of an earlier day. "As for me, I am very old. I and my dead will stay together at home."

The man fled, and left her to her choice.

The great curled flames and the livid vapours closed around her; she never moved. The death was fierce, but swift, and even in death she and the one whom she had loved and reared were not divided. The end soon came. From hill to hill the Berceau de Dieu broke into flames. The village was a lake of fire, into which the statue of the Christ, burning and reeling, fell. Some few peasants, with their wives and children, fled to the woods, and there escaped one torture to perish more slowly of cold and famine. All other things perished. The rapid stream of the flame licked up all there was in its path. The bare trees raised their leafless branches, on fire at a thousand points. The stores of corn and fruit were lapped by millions of crimson tongues. The pigeons flew screaming from their roosts, and sank into the smoke. The dogs were suffocated on the thresholds they had guarded all their lives. The sheep ran bleating with the wool burning on their living bodies. The little caged birds fluttered helpless, and then dropped, scorched to cinders. The aged and the sick were stifled in their beds. All things perished.

The Berceau de Dieu was as one vast furnace, in which every living creature was caught and consumed and changed to ashes. The tide of war has rolled on, and left it a blackened waste, a smoking ruin, wherein not so much as a mouse may creep or a bird may nestle. It is gone, and its place can know it nevermore.

Nevermore. But who is there to care? It was but as a leaf which the great storm swept away as it passed.

THE TRAVELLER'S STORY OF A TERRIBLY STRANGE BED

PROLOGUE TO THE FIRST STORY

Before I begin, by the aid of my wife's patient attention and ready pen, to relate any of the stories which I have heard at various times from persons whose likenesses I have been employed to take, it will not be amiss if I try to secure the reader's interest in the following pages by briefly explaining how I became possessed of the narrative matter which they contain.

Of myself I have nothing to say, but that I have followed the profession of a travelling portrait-painter for the last fifteen years. The pursuit of my calling has not only led me all through England, but has taken me twice to Scotland and once to Ireland. In moving from district to district, I am never guided beforehand by any settled plan. Sometimes the letters of recommendation which I get from persons who are satisfied with the work I have done for them determine the direction in which I travel. Sometimes I hear of a new neighbourhood in which there is no resident artist of ability, and remove thither on speculation. Sometimes my friends among the picture-dealers say a good word on my behalf to their rich customers, and so pave the way for me in the large towns. Sometimes my prosperous and famous brother artists, hearing of small commissions which it is not worth their while to accept, mention my name, and procure me introductions to pleasant country houses. Thus I get on, now in one way and now in another, not winning a reputation or making a fortune, but happier, perhaps, on the whole, than many men who have got both the one and the other. So, at least, I try to think now, though I started in my youth with as high an ambition as the best of them. Thank God, it is not my business here to speak of past times and their disappointments. A twinge of the old hopeless heartache comes over me sometimes still, when I think of my student days.

One peculiarity of my present way of life is, that it brings me into contact with all sorts of characters. I almost feel, by this time, as if I had painted every civilised variety of the human race. Upon the whole, my experience of the world, rough as it has been, has not taught me to think unkindly of my fellow-creatures. I have certainly received such treatment at the hands of some of my sitters as I could not describe without saddening and shocking any kind-hearted reader; but, taking one year and one place with another, I have cause to remember with gratitude and respect, sometimes even with friendship and affection, a very large proportion of the numerous persons who have employed me.

Some of the results of my experience are curious in a moral point of view. For example, I have found women almost uniformly less delicate in asking me about my terms, and less generous in remunerating me for my services, than men. On the other hand, men, within my knowledge, are decidedly vainer of their personal attractions, and more vexatiously anxious to have them done full justice to on canvas, than women. Taking both sexes together, I have found young people, for the most part, more gentle, more reasonable, and more considerate than old. And, summing up, in a general way, my experience of different ranks (which extends, let me premise, all the way down from peers to publicans), I have met with most of my formal and ungracious receptions among rich people of uncertain social standing; the highest classes and the lowest among my employers almost always contrive - in widely different ways, of course - to make me feel at home as soon as I enter their houses.

The one great obstacle that I have to contend against in the practice of my profession is not, as some persons may imagine, the difficulty of making my sitters keep their heads still while I paint them, but the difficulty of getting them to preserve the natural look and the everyday peculiarities of dress and manner. People will assume an expression, will brush up their hair, will correct any little characteristic carelessness in their apparel - will, in short, when they want to have their likenesses taken, look as if they were sitting for their pictures. If I paint them under these artificial circumstances, I fail, of course, to present them in their habitual aspect; and my portrait, as a necessary consequence, disappoints everybody, the sitter always included. When we wish to judge of a man's character by his handwriting, we want his customary scrawl dashed off with his common workaday pen, not his best small text traced laboriously with the finest procurable crow-quill point. So it is with portrait-painting, which is, after all, nothing but a right reading of the externals of character recognisably presented to the view of others.

Experience, after repeated trials, has proved to me that

the only way of getting sitters who persist in assuming a set look to resume their habitual expression is to lead them into talking about some subject in which they are greatly interested. If I can only beguile them into speaking earnestly, no matter on what topic, I am sure of recovering their natural expression; sure of seeing all the little precious every-day peculiarities of the man or woman peep out, one after another, quite unawares. The long maundering stories about nothing, the wearisome recitals of petty grievances, the local anecdotes unrelieved by the faintest suspicion of anything like general interest, which I have been condemned to hear, as a consequence of thawing the ice off the features of formal sitters by the method just described, would fill hundreds of volumes and promote the repose of thousands of readers. On the other hand, if I have suffered under the tediousness of the many, I have not been without my compensating gains from the wisdom and experience of the few. To some of my sitters I have been indebted for information which has enlarged my mind, to some for advice which has lightened my heart, to some for narratives of strange adventure which riveted my attention at the time, which have served to interest and amuse my fireside circle for many years past, and which are now, I would fain hope, destined to make kind friends for me among a wider audience than any that I have yet addressed.

Singularly enough, almost all the best stories that I have heard from my sitters have been told by accident. I only remember two cases in which a story was volunteered to me; and, although I have often tried the experiment, I cannot call to mind even a single instance in which leading questions (as lawyers call them) on my part, addressed to a sitter, ever produced any result worth recording. Over and over again I have been disastrously successful in encouraging dull people to weary me. But the clever people who have something interesting to say seem, so far as I have observed them, to acknowledge no other stimulant than chance. For every story, excepting one, I have been indebted, in the first instance, to the capricious influence of the same chance. Something my sitter has seen about me, something I have remarked in my sitter, or in the room in which I take the likeness, or in the neighbourhood through which I pass on my way to work, has suggested the necessary association, or has started the right train of recollections, and then the story appeared to begin of its own accord. Occasionally the most casual notice, on my part, of some very unpromising object has smoothed the way for the relation of a long and interesting narrative. I first heard one of the most dramatic stories merely through being carelessly inquisitive to know the history of a stuffed poodle-dog.

It is thus not without reason that I lay some stress on the desirableness of prefacing the following narrative by a brief account of the curious manner in which I became possessed of it. As to my capacity for repeating the story correctly, I can answer for it that my memory may be trusted. I may claim it as a merit, because it is, after all, a mechanical one, that I forget nothing, and that I can call long-past conversations and events as readily to my recollection as if they had happened but a few weeks ago. Of two things at least I feel tolerably certain before-hand, in meditating over its contents: first, that I can repeat correctly all that I have heard; and, secondly, that I have never missed anything worth hearing when my sitters were addressing me on an interesting subject. Although I cannot take the lead in talking while I am engaged in painting, I can listen while others speak, and work all the better for it.

So much in the way of general preface to the pages for which I am about to ask the reader's attention. Let me now advance to particulars, and describe how I came to hear the story. I begin with it because it is the story that I have oftenest "rehearsed," to borrow a phrase from the stage. Wherever I go, I am sooner or later sure to tell it. Only last night I was persuaded into repeating it once more by the inhabitants of the farm-house in which I am now staying.

Not many years ago, on returning from a short holiday visit to a friend settled in Paris, I found professional letters awaiting me at my agent's in London, which required my immediate presence in Liverpool. Without stopping to unpack, I proceeded by the first conveyance to my new destination; and, calling at the picture-dealer's shop where portrait-painting engagements were received for me, found to my great satisfaction that I had remunerative employment in prospect, in and about Liverpool, for at least two months to come. I was putting up my letters in high spirits, and was just leaving the picture-dealer's shop to look out for comfortable lodgings, when I was met at the door by the landlord of one of the largest hotels in Liverpool - an old acquaintance whom I had known as manager of a tavern in London in my student days.

"Mr. Kerby!" he exclaimed, in great astonishment. "What an unexpected meeting! the last man in the world whom I expected to see, and yet the very man whose services I want to make use of!"

"What! more work for me?" said I. "Are all the people

in Liverpool going to have their portraits painted?"

"I only know of one," replied the landlord, "a gentleman staying at my hotel, who wants a chalk drawing done of him. I was on my way here to inquire for any artist whom our picture-dealing friend could recommend. How glad I am that I met you before I had committed myself to employing a stranger!"

"Is this likeness wanted at once?" I asked, thinking of the number of engagements that I had already got in my pocket.

"Immediately - to-day - this very hour, if possible," said the landlord. "Mr. Faulkner, the gentleman I am speaking of, was to have sailed yesterday for the Brazils from this place; but the wind shifted last night to the wrong quarter, and he came ashore again this morning. He may, of course, be detained here for some time; but he may also be called on board ship at half an hour's notice, if the wind shifts back again in the right direction. This uncertainty makes it a matter of importance that the likeness should be begun immediately. Undertake it if you possibly can, for Mr. Faulkner is a liberal gentleman, who is sure to give you your own terms."

I reflected for a minute or two. The portrait was only wanted in chalk, and would not take long; besides, I might finish it in the evening, if my other engagements pressed hard upon me in the daytime. Why not leave my luggage at the picture-dealer's, put off looking for lodgings till night, and secure the new commission boldly by going back at once with the landlord to the hotel? I decided on following this course almost as soon as the idea occurred to me; put my chalks in my pocket, and a sheet of drawing-paper in the first of my portfolios that came to hand; and so presented myself before Mr. Faulkner, ready to take his likeness, literally at five minutes' notice.

I found him a very pleasant, intelligent man, young and handsome. He had been a great traveller, had visited all the wonders of the East, and was now about to explore the wilds of the vast South American continent. Thus much he told me good-humouredly and unconstrainedly while I was preparing my drawing materials.

As soon as I had put him in the right light and position, and had seated myself opposite to him, he changed the subject of conversation, and asked me, a little confusedly as I thought, if it was not a customary practice among portrait-painters to gloss over the faults in their sitters' faces, and to make as much as possible of any good points which their features might possess.

"Certainly," I answered. "You have described the whole art and mystery of successful portrait-painting in a few words."

"May I beg, then," said he, "that you will depart from the usual practice in my case, and draw me with all my defects, exactly as I am? The fact is," he went on, after a moment's pause, "the likeness you are now preparing to take is intended for my mother. my roving disposition makes me a great anxiety to her, and she parted from me this last time very sadly and unwillingly. I don't know how the idea came into my head, but it struck me this morning that I could not better employ the time while I was delayed here on shore than by getting my likeness done to send to her as a keepsake. She has no portrait of me since I was a child, and she is sure to value a drawing of me more than anything else I could send to her. I only trouble you with this explanation to prove that I am really sincere in my wish to be drawn unflatteringly, exactly as I am."

Secretly respecting and admiring him for what he had just said, I promised that his directions should be implicitly followed, and began to work immediately. Before I had pursued my occupation for ten minutes, the conversation began to flag, and the usual obstacle to my success with a sitter gradually set itself up between us. Quite unconsciously, of course, Mr. Faulkner stiffened his neck, shut his mouth, and contracted his eyebrows - evidently under the impression that he was facilitating the process of taking his portrait by making his face as like a lifeless mask as possible. All traces of his natural animated expression were fast disappearing, and he was beginning to change into a heavy and rather melancholy-looking man.

This complete alteration was of no great consequence so long as I was only engaged in drawing the outline of his face and the general form of his features. I accordingly worked on doggedly for more than an hour; then left off to point my chalks again, and to give my sitter a few minutes' rest. Thus far the likeness had not suffered through Mr. Faulkner's unfortunate notion of the right way of sitting for his portrait; but the time of difficulty, as I well knew, was to come. It was impossible for me to think of putting any expression into the drawing unless I could contrive some means, when he resumed his chair, of making him look like himself again. "I will talk to him about foreign parts," thought I, "and try if I can't make him forget that he is sitting for his picture in that way."

While I was pointing my chalks, Mr. Faulkner was walking up and down the room. He chanced to see the portfolio I had brought with me leaning against the wall, and asked if there were any sketches in it. I told him there were a few which I had made during my recent stay in Paris. "In Paris?" he repeated, with a look of interest; "may I see them?"

I gave him the permission he asked as a matter of course. Sitting down, he took the portfolio on his knee, and began to look through it. He turned over the first five sketches rapidly enough; but when he came to the sixth I saw his face flush directly, and observed that he took the drawing out of the portfolio, carried it to the window, and remained silently absorbed in the contemplation of it for full five minutes. After that he turned round to me, and asked very anxiously if I had any objection to parting with that sketch.

It was the least interesting drawing of the collection - merely a view in one of the streets running by the backs of the houses in the Palais Royal. Some four or five of these houses were comprised in the view, which was of no particular use to me in any way, and which was too valueless, as a work of art, for me to think of selling it. I begged his acceptance of it at once. He thanked me quite warmly; and then, seeing that I looked a little surprised at the odd selection he had made from my sketches, laughingly asked me if I could guess why he had been so anxious to become possessed of the view which I had given him.

"Probably," I answered, "there is some remarkable historical association connected with that street at the back of the Palais Royal, of which I am ignorant."

"No," said Mr. Faulkner; "at least none that I know of. The only association connected with the place in my mind is a purely personal association. Look at this house in your drawing - the house with the water-pipe running down it from top to bottom. I once passed a night there - a night I shall never forget to the day of my death. I have had some awkward travelling adventures in my time; but that adventure! Well, never mind, suppose we begin the sitting. I make but a bad return for your kindness in giving me the sketch by thus wasting your time in mere talk."

"Come! come!" thought I, as he went back to the sitter's chair, "I shall see your natural expression on your face if I can only get you to talk about that adventure." It was easy enough to lead him in the right direction. At the first hint from me, he returned to the subject of the house in the back street. Without, I hope, showing any undue curiosity, I contrived to let him see that I felt a deep interest in everything he now said. After two or three preliminary hesitations, he at last, to my great joy, fairly started on the narrative of his adventure. In the interest of his subject he soon completely forgot that he was sitting for his portrait, - the very expression that I wanted came over his face, - and my drawing proceeded toward completion, in the right direction, and to the best purpose. At every fresh touch I felt more and more certain that I was now getting the better of my grand difficulty; and I enjoyed the additional gratification of having my work lightened by the recital of a true story, which possessed, in my estimation, all the excitement of the most exciting romance.

This, as I recollect it, is how Mr. Faulkner told me his adventure.

THE TRAVELLER'S STORY OF A TERRIBLY STRANGE BED

Shortly after my education at college was finished, I happened to be staying at Paris with an English friend. We were both young men then, and lived, I am afraid, rather a wild life, in the delightful city of our sojourn. One night we were idling about the neighbourhood of the Palais Royal, doubtful to what amusement we should next betake ourselves. My friend proposed a visit to Frascati's; but his suggestion was not to my taste. I knew Frascati's, as the French saying is, by heart; had lost and won plenty of five-franc pieces there, merely for amusement's sake, until it was amusement no longer, and was thoroughly tired, in fact, of all the ghastly respectabilities of such a social anomaly as a respectable gambling-house. "For Heaven's sake," said I to my friend, "let us go somewhere where we can see a little genuine, blackguard, poverty-stricken gaming with no false gingerbread glitter thrown over it all. Let us get away from fashionable Frascati's, to a house where they don't mind letting in a man with a ragged coat, or a man with no coat, ragged or otherwise." "Very well," said my friend, "we needn't go out of the Palais Royal to find the sort of company you want. Here's the place just before us; as blackguard a place, by all report, as you could possibly wish to see." In another minute we arrived at the door and entered the house, the back of which you have drawn in your sketch.

When we got upstairs, and had left our hats and sticks

with the doorkeeper, we were admitted into the chief gambling-room. We did not find many people assembled there. But, few as the men were who looked up at us on our entrance, they were all types - lamentably true types - of their respective classes.

We had come to see blackguards; but these men were something worse. There is a comic side, more or less appreciable, in all blackguardism - here there was nothing but tragedy - mute, weird tragedy. The quiet in the room was horrible. The thin, haggard, long-haired young man, whose sunken eyes fiercely watched the turning up of the cards, never spoke; the flabby, fat-faced, pimply player, who pricked his piece of pasteboard perseveringly, to register how often black won, and how often red - never spoke; the dirty, wrinkled old man, with the vulture eyes and the darned great-coat, who had lost his last sou, and still looked on desperately, after he could play no longer - never spoke. Even the voice of the croupier sounded as if it were strangely dulled and thickened in the atmosphere of the room. I had entered the place to laugh, but the spectacle before me was something to weep over. I soon found it necessary to take refuge in excitement from the depression of spirits which was fast stealing on me. Unfortunately I sought the nearest excitement, by going to the table and beginning to play. Still more unfortunately, as the event will show, I won - won prodigiously; won incredibly; won at such a rate that the regular players at the table crowded round me; and staring at my stakes with hungry, superstitious eyes, whispered to one another that the English stranger was going to break the bank.

The game was Rouge et Noir. I had played at it in every city in Europe, without, however, the care or the wish to study the Theory of Chances - that philosopher's stone of all gamblers! And a gambler, in the strict sense of the word, I had never been. I was heart-whole from the corroding passion for play. My gaming was a mere idle amusement. I never resorted to it by necessity, because I never knew what it was to want money. I never practised it so incessantly as to lose more than I could afford, or to gain more than I could coolly pocket without being thrown off my balance by my good luck. In short, I had hitherto frequented gambling-tables - just as I frequented ball-rooms and opera-houses - because they amused me, and because I had nothing better to do with my leisure hours.

But on this occasion it was very different - now, for the first time in my life, I felt what the passion for play really was. My success first bewildered, and then, in the most literal meaning of the word, intoxicated me. Incredible as it may appear, it is nevertheless true, that I only lost when I attempted to estimate chances, and played according to previous calculation. If I left everything to luck, and staked without any care or consideration, I was sure to win - to win in the face of every recognized probability in favour of the bank. At first some of the men present ventured their money safely enough on my colour; but I speedily increased my stakes to sums which they dared not risk. One after another they left off playing, and breathlessly looked on at my game.

Still, time after time, I staked higher and higher, and still won. The excitement in the room rose to fever pitch. The silence was interrupted by a deep-muttered chorus of oaths and exclamations in different languages, every time the gold was shovelled across to my side of the table - even the imperturbable croupier dashed his rake on the floor in a (French) fury of astonishment at my success. But one man present preserved his self-possession, and that man was my friend. He came to my side, and whispering in English, begged me to leave the place, satisfied with what I had already gained. I must do him the justice to say that he repeated his warnings and entreaties several times, and only left me and went away after I had rejected his advice (I was to all intents and purposes gambling drunk) in terms which rendered it impossible for him to address me again that night.

Shortly after he had gone, a hoarse voice behind me cried: "Permit me, my dear sir - permit me to restore to their proper place two napoleons which you have dropped. Wonderful luck, sir! I pledge you my word of honour, as an old soldier, in the course of my long experience in this sort of thing, I never saw such luck as yours - never! Go on, sir - Sacre mille bombes! Go on boldly, and break the bank!"

I turned round and saw, nodding and smiling at me with inveterate civility, a tall man, dressed in a frogged and braided surtout. If I had been in my senses, I should have considered him, personally, as being rather a suspicious specimen of an old soldier. He had goggling bloodshot eyes, mangy moustaches, and a broken nose. His voice betrayed a barrack-room intonation of the worst order, and he had the dirtiest pair of hands I ever saw - even in France. These little personal peculiarities exercised, however, no repelling influence on me. In the mad excitement, the reckless triumph of that moment, I was ready to "fraternize" with anybody who encouraged me in my game. I accepted the old soldier's offered pinch of snuff;

clapped him on the back, and swore he was the honestest fellow in the world - the most glorious relic of the Grand Army that I had ever met with. "Go on!" cried my military friend, snapping his fingers in ecstasy - "Go on, and win! Break the bank - Mille tonnerres! my gallant English comrade, break the bank!"

And I did go on - went on at such a rate, that in another quarter of an hour the croupier called out, "Gentlemen, the bank has discontinued for to-night." All the notes, and all the gold in that "bank" now lay in a heap under my hands; the whole floating capital of the gambling-house was waiting to pour into my pockets!

"Tie up the money in your pocket-handkerchief, my worthy sir," said the old soldier, as I wildly plunged my hands into my heap of gold. "Tie it up, as we used to tie up a bit of dinner in the Grand Army; your winnings are too heavy for any breeches-pockets that ever were sewed. There! that's it - shovel them in, notes and all! Credie! what luck! Stop! another napoleon on the floor! Ah! sacre petit polisson de Napoleon! have I found thee at last? Now then, sir - two tight double knots each way with your honourable permission, and the money's safe. Feel it! feel it, fortunate sir! hard and round as a cannon-ball - Ah, bah! if they had only fired such cannon-balls at us at Austerlitz - nom d'une pipe! if they only had! And now, as an ancient grenadier, as an ex-brave of the French army, what remains for me to do? I ask what? Simply this: to entreat my valued English friend to drink a bottle of champagne with me, and toast the goddess Fortune in foaming goblets before we part!"

"Excellent ex-brave! Convivial ancient grenadier!

Champagne by all means! An English cheer for an old soldier! Hurrah! hurrah! Another English cheer for the goddess Fortune! Hurrah! hurrah! hurrah!"

"Bravo! the Englishman; the amiable, gracious Englishman, in whose veins circulates the vivacious blood of France! Another glass? Ah, bah! - the bottle is empty! Never mind! Vive le vin! I, the old soldier, order another bottle, and half a pound of bonbons with it!"

"No, no, ex-brave; never - ancient grenadier! Your bottle last time; my bottle this. Behold it! Toast away! The French Army! the great Napoleon! the present company! the croupier! the honest croupier's wife and daughters - if he has any! the Ladies generally! everybody in the world!"

By the time the second bottle of champagne was emptied, I felt as if I had been drinking liquid fire - my brain seemed all aflame. No excess in wine had ever had this effect on me before in my life. Was it the result of a stimulant acting upon my system when I was in a highly excited state? Was my stomach in a particularly disordered condition? Or was the champagne amazingly strong?

"Ex-brave of the French Army!" cried I, in a mad state of exhilaration, "I am on fire! how are you? You have set me on fire. Do you hear, my hero of Austerlitz? Let us have a third bottle of champagne to put the flame out!"

The old soldier wagged his head, rolled his goggle-eyes, until I expected to see them slip out of their sockets; placed his dirty forefinger by the side of his broken nose; solemnly ejaculated "Coffee!" and immediately ran off into an inner room.

The word pronounced by the eccentric veteran seemed to have a magical effect on the rest of the company present. With one accord they all rose to depart. Probably they had expected to profit by my intoxication; but finding that my new friend was benevolently bent on preventing me from getting dead drunk, had now abandoned all hope of thriving pleasantly on my winnings. Whatever their motive might be, at any rate they went away in a body. When the old soldier returned, and sat down again opposite to me at the table, we had the room to ourselves. I could see the croupier, in a sort of vestibule which opened out of it, eating his supper in solitude. The silence was now deeper than ever.

A sudden change, too, had come over the "ex-brave". He assumed a portentously solemn look; and when he spoke to me again, his speech was ornamented by no oaths, enforced by no finger-snapping, enlivened by no apostrophes or exclamations.

"Listen, my dear sir," said he, in mysteriously confidential tones - "listen to an old soldier's advice. I have been to the mistress of the house (a very charming woman, with a genius for cookery!) to impress on her the necessity of making us some particularly strong and good coffee. You must drink this coffee in order to get rid of your little amiable exaltation of spirits before you think of going home – you must , my good and gracious friend! With all that money to take home to-night, it is a sacred duty to yourself to have your wits about you. You are known to be a winner to an enormous extent by several gentlemen present to-night, who, in a certain point of view, are very worthy and excellent fellows; but they are mortal men, my dear sir, and they have their amiable weaknesses. Need I say more? Ah, no, no! you understand me! Now, this is what you must do - send for a cabriolet when you feel quite well again - draw up all the windows when you get into it - and tell the driver to take you home only through the large and well-lighted thoroughfares. Do this; and you and your money will be safe. Do this; and to-morrow you will thank an old soldier for giving you a word of honest advice."

Just as the ex-brave ended his oration in very lachrymose tones, the coffee came in, ready poured out in two cups. My attentive friend handed me one of the cups with a bow. I was parched with thirst, and drank it off at a draught. Almost instantly afterwards, I was seized with a fit of giddiness, and felt more completely intoxicated than ever. The room whirled round and round furiously; the old soldier seemed to be regularly bobbing up and down before me like the piston of a steam-engine. I was half deafened by a violent singing in my ears; a feeling of utter bewilderment, helplessness, idiocy, overcame me. I rose from my chair, holding on by the table to keep my balance; and stammered out that I felt dreadfully unwell - so unwell that I did not know how I was to get home.

"My dear friend," answered the old soldier - and even his voice seemed to be bobbing up and down as he spoke - "my dear friend, it would be madness to go home in your state; you would be sure to lose your money; you might be robbed and murdered with the greatest ease. I am going to sleep here; do you sleep here, too - they make up capital beds in this house -

take one; sleep off the effects of the wine, and go home safely with your winnings to-morrow - to-morrow, in broad daylight."

I had but two ideas left: one, that I must never let go hold of my handkerchief full of money; the other, that I must lie down somewhere immediately, and fall off into a comfortable sleep. So I agreed to the proposal about the bed, and took the offered arm of the old soldier, carrying my money with my disengaged hand. Preceded by the croupier, we passed along some passages and up a flight of stairs into the bedroom which I was to occupy. The ex-brave shook me warmly by the hand, proposed that we should breakfast together, and then, followed by the croupier, left me for the night.

I ran to the wash-hand stand; drank some of the water in my jug; poured the rest out, and plunged my face into it; then sat down in a chair and tried to compose myself. I soon felt better. The change for my lungs, from the fetid atmosphere of the gambling-room to the cool air of the apartment I now occupied, the almost equally refreshing change for my eyes, from the glaring gaslights of the "salon" to the dim, quiet flicker of one bedroom candle, aided wonderfully the restorative effects of cold water. The giddiness left me, and I began to feel a little like a reasonable being again. My first thought was of the risk of sleeping all night in a gambling-house; my second, of the still greater risk of trying to get out after the house was closed, and of going home alone at night through the streets of Paris with a large sum of money about me. I had slept in worse places than this on my travels; so I determined to lock, bolt, and barricade my door, and take my chance till the next morning.

Accordingly, I secured myself against all intrusion; looked under the bed, and into the cupboard; tried the fastening of the window; and then, satisfied that I had taken every proper precaution, pulled off my upper clothing, put my light, which was a dim one, on the hearth among a feathery litter of wood-ashes, and got into bed, with the handkerchief full of money under my pillow.

I soon felt not only that I could not go to sleep, but that I could not even close my eyes. I was wide awake, and in a high fever. Every nerve in my body trembled - every one of my senses seemed to be preternaturally sharpened. I tossed and rolled, and tried every kind of position, and perseveringly sought out the cold corners of the bed, and all to no purpose. Now I thrust my arms over the clothes; now I poked them under the clothes; now I violently shot my legs straight out down to the bottom of the bed; now I convulsively coiled them up as near my chin as they would go; now I shook out my crumpled pillow, changed it to the cool side, patted it flat, and lay down quietly on my back; now I fiercely doubled it in two, set it up on end, thrust it against the board of the bed, and tried a sitting posture. Every effort was in vain; I groaned with vexation as I felt that I was in for a sleepless night.

What could I do? I had no book to read. And yet, unless I found out some method of diverting my mind, I felt certain that I was in the condition to imagine all sorts of horrors; to rack my brain with forebodings of every possible and impossible danger; in short, to pass the night in suffering all conceivable varieties of nervous terror.

I raised myself on my elbow, and looked about the

room - which was brightened by a lovely moonlight pouring straight through the window - to see if it contained any pictures or ornaments that I could at all clearly distinguish. While my eyes wandered from wall to wall, a remembrance of Le Maistre's delightful little book, "Voyage autour de ma Chambre," occurred to me. I resolved to imitate the French author, and find occupation and amusement enough to relieve the tedium of my wakefulness, by making a mental inventory of every article of furniture I could see, and by following up to their sources the multitude of associations which even a chair, a table, or a wash-hand stand may be made to call forth.

In the nervous unsettled state of my mind at that moment, I found it much easier to make my inventory than to make my reflections, and thereupon soon gave up all hope of thinking in Le Maistre's fanciful track - or, indeed, of thinking at all. I looked about the room at the different articles of furniture, and did nothing more.

There was, first, the bed I was lying in; a four-post bed, of all things in the world to meet with in Paris - yes, a thoroughly clumsy British four-poster, with the regular top lined with chintz - the regular fringed valance all round - the regular stifling, unwholesome curtains, which I remembered having mechanically drawn back against the posts without particularly noticing the bed when I first got into the room. Then there was the marble-topped wash-hand stand, from which the water I had spilled, in my hurry to pour it out, was still dripping, slowly and more slowly, on to the brick floor. Then two small chairs, with my coat, waistcoat, and trousers flung on them. Then a large elbow-chair covered with dirty-white dimity, with my cravat and shirt collar thrown over the back. Then a chest of drawers with two of the brass handles off, and a tawdry, broken china inkstand placed on it by way of ornament for the top. Then the dressing-table, adorned by a very small looking-glass, and a very large pincushion. Then the window - an unusually large window. Then a dark old picture, which the feeble candle dimly showed me. It was a picture of a fellow in a high Spanish hat, crowned with a plume of towering feathers. A swarthy, sinister ruffian, looking upward, shading his eyes with his hand, and looking intently upward - it might be at some tall gallows at which he was going to be hanged. At any rate, he had the appearance of thoroughly deserving it.

This picture put a kind of constraint upon me to look upward too - at the top of the bed. It was a gloomy and not an interesting object, and I looked back at the picture. I counted the feathers in the man's hat - they stood out in relief - three white, two green. I observed the crown of his hat, which was of conical shape, according to the fashion supposed to have been favoured by Guido Fawkes. I wondered what he was looking up at. It couldn't be at the stars; such a desperado was neither astrologer nor astronomer. It must be at the high gallows, and he was going to be hanged presently. Would the executioner come into possession of his conical crowned hat and plume of feathers? I counted the feathers again - three white, two green.

While I still lingered over this very improving and intellectual employment, my thoughts insensibly began to wander. The moonlight shining into the room reminded me of a certain moonlight night in England - the night after a picnic party in a Welsh valley. Every incident of the drive homeward, through lovely scenery, which the moonlight made lovelier than ever, came back to my remembrance, though I had never given the picnic a thought for years; though, if I had tried to recollect it, I could certainly have recalled little or nothing of that scene long past. Of all the wonderful faculties that help to tell us we are immortal, which speaks the sublime truth more eloquently than memory? Here was I, in a strange house of the most suspicious character, in a situation of uncertainty, and even of peril, which might seem to make the cool exercise of my recollection almost out of the question; nevertheless, remembering, quite involuntarily, places, people, conversations, minute circumstances of every kind, which I had thought forgotten for ever; which I could not possibly have recalled at will, even under the most favourable auspices. And what cause had produced in a moment the whole of this strange, complicated, mysterious effect? Nothing but some rays of moonlight shining in at my bedroom window.

I was still thinking of the picnic - of our merriment on the drive home - of the sentimental young lady who would quote "Childe Harold" because it was moonlight. I was absorbed by these past scenes and past amusements, when, in an instant, the thread on which my memories hung snapped asunder; my attention immediately came back to present things more vividly than ever, and I found myself, I neither knew why nor wherefore, looking hard at the picture again.

Looking for what?

Good God! the man had pulled his hat down on his brows! No! the hat itself was gone! Where was the conical crown? Where the feathers - three white, two green? Not there! In place of the hat and feathers, what dusky object was it that now hid his forehead, his eyes, his shading hand?

Was the bed moving?

I turned on my back and looked up. Was I mad? drunk? dreaming? Giddy again? or was the top of the bed really moving down - sinking slowly, regularly, silently, horribly, right down throughout the whole of its length and breadth - right down upon me, as I lay underneath?

My blood seemed to stand still. A deadly paralysing coldness stole all over me as I turned my head round on the pillow and determined to test whether the bedtop was really moving or not, by keeping my eye on the man in the picture.

The next look in that direction was enough. The dull, black, frowzy outline of the valance above me was within an inch of being parallel with his waist. I still looked breathlessly. And steadily and slowly - very slowly - I saw the figure, and the line of frame below the figure, vanish, as the valance moved down before it.

I am, constitutionally, anything but timid. I have been on more than one occasion in peril of my life, and have not lost my self-possession for an instant; but when the conviction first settled on my mind that the bed-top was really moving, was steadily and continuously sinking down upon me, I looked up shuddering, helpless, panic-stricken, beneath the hideous machinery for murder, which was advancing closer and closer to suffocate me where I lay.

I looked up, motionless, speechless, breathless. The candle, fully spent, went out; but the moonlight still brightened the room. Down and down, without pausing and without sounding, came the bedtop, and still my panic terror seemed to bind me faster and faster to the mattress on which I lay - down and down it sank, till the dusty odour from the lining of the canopy came stealing into my nostrils.

At that final moment the instinct of self-preservation startled me out of my trance, and I moved at last. There was just room for me to roll myself sideways off the bed. As I dropped noiselessly to the floor, the edge of the murderous canopy touched me on the shoulder.

Without stopping to draw my breath, without wiping the cold sweat from my face, I rose instantly on my knees to watch the bedtop. I was literally spellbound by it. If I had heard footsteps behind me, I could not have turned round; if a means of escape had been miraculously provided for me, I could not have moved to take advantage of it. The whole life in me was, at that moment, concentrated in my eyes.

It descended - the whole canopy, with the fringe round it, came down - down - close down; so close that there was not room now to squeeze my finger between the bedtop and the bed. I felt at the sides, and discovered that what had appeared to me from beneath to be the ordinary light canopy of a four-post bed was in reality a thick, broad mattress, the substance of which was concealed by the valance and its fringe. I looked up and saw the four posts rising hideously bare. In the middle of the bedtop was a huge wooden screw that had evidently worked it down through a hole in the ceiling, just as ordinary presses are worked down on the substance selected for compression. The frightful apparatus moved without making the faintest noise. There had been no creaking as it came down; there was now not the faintest sound from the room above. Amid a dead and awful silence I beheld before me - in the nineteenth century, and in the civilized capital of France - such a machine for secret murder by suffocation as might have existed in the worst days of the Inquisition, in the lonely inns among the Harz Mountains, in the mysterious tribunals of Westphalia! Still, as I looked on it, I could not move, I could hardly breathe, but I began to recover the power of thinking, and in a moment I discovered the murderous conspiracy framed against me in all its horror.

My cup of coffee had been drugged, and drugged too strongly. I had been saved from being smothered by having taken an overdose of some narcotic. How I had chafed and fretted at the fever-fit which had preserved my life by keeping me awake! How recklessly I had confided myself to the two wretches who had led me into this room, determined, for the sake of my winnings, to kill me in my sleep by the surest and most horrible contrivance for secretly accomplishing my destruction! How many men, winners like me, had slept, as I had proposed to sleep, in that bed, and had never been seen or heard of more! I shuddered at the bare idea of it.

But, ere long, all thought was again suspended by the sight of the murderous canopy moving once more. After it had remained on the bed - as nearly as I could guess - about ten minutes, it began to move up again. The villains who worked it from above evidently believed that their purpose was now accomplished. Slowly and silently, as it had descended, that horrible bedtop rose towards its former place. When it reached the upper extremities of the four posts, it reached the ceiling, too. Neither hole nor screw could be seen; the bed became in appearance an ordinary bed again - the canopy an ordinary canopy - even to the most suspicious eyes.

Now, for the first time, I was able to move - to rise from my knees - to dress myself in my upper clothing - and to consider of how I should escape. If I betrayed by the smallest noise that the attempt to suffocate me had failed, I was certain to be murdered. Had I made any noise already? I listened intently, looking towards the door.

No! no footsteps in the passage outside - no sound of a tread, light or heavy, in the room above - absolute silence everywhere. Besides locking and bolting my door, I had moved an old wooden chest against it, which I had found under the bed. To remove this chest (my blood ran cold as I thought of what its contents might be!) without making some disturbance was impossible; and, moreover, to think of escaping through the house, now barred up for the night, was sheer insanity. Only one chance was left me - the window. I stole to it on tiptoe.

My bedroom was on the first floor, above an entresol, and looked into a back street. I raised my hand to open the window, knowing that on that action hung, by the merest hairbreadth, my chance of safety. They keep vigilant watch in a house of murder. If any part of the frame cracked, if the hinge creaked, I was a lost man! It must have occupied me at least five minutes, reckoning by time - five hours, reckoning by suspense - to open that window. I succeeded in doing it silently -

in doing it with all the dexterity of a house-breaker - and then looked down into the street. To leap the distance beneath me would be almost certain destruction! Next, I looked round at the sides of the house. Down the left side ran a thick water-pipe - it passed close by the outer edge of the window. The moment I saw the pipe I knew I was saved. My breath came and went freely for the first time since I had seen the canopy of the bed moving down upon me!

To some men the means of escape which I had discovered might have seemed difficult and dangerous enough - to me the prospect of slipping down the pipe into the street did not suggest even a thought of peril. I had always been accustomed, by the practice of gymnastics, to keep up my school-boy powers as a daring and expert climber; and knew that my head, hands, and feet would serve me faithfully in any hazards of ascent or descent. I had already got one leg over the window-sill, when I remembered the handkerchief filled with money under my pillow. I could well have afforded to leave it behind me, but I was revengefully determined that the miscreants of the gambling-house should miss their plunder as well as their victim. So I went back to the bed and tied the heavy handkerchief at my back by my cravat.

Just as I had made it tight and fixed it in a comfortable place, I thought I heard a sound of breathing outside the door. The chill feeling of horror ran through me again as I listened. No! dead silence still in the passage - I had only heard the night air blowing softly into the room. The next moment I was on the window-sill, and the next I had a firm grip on the water-pipe with my hands and knees.

I slid down into the street easily and quietly, as I thought I should, and immediately set off at the top of my speed to a branch "prefecture" of Police, which I knew was situated in the immediate neighbourhood. A "subprefect," and several picked men among his subordinates, happened to be up, maturing, I believe, some scheme for discovering the perpetrator of a mysterious murder which all Paris was talking of just then. When I began my story, in a breathless hurry and in very bad French, I could see that the subprefect suspected me of being a drunken Englishman who had robbed somebody; but he soon altered his opinion as I went on, and before I had anything like concluded, he shoved all the papers before him into a drawer, put on his hat, supplied me with another (for I was bare-headed), ordered a file of soldiers, desired his expert followers to get ready all sorts of tools for breaking open doors and ripping up brick flooring, and took my arm, in the most friendly and familiar manner possible, to lead me with him out of the house. I will venture to say that when the subprefect was a little boy, and was taken for the first time to the play, he was not half as much pleased as he was now at the job in prospect for him at the gambling-house!

Away we went through the streets, the subprefect cross-examining and congratulating me in the same breath as we marched at the head of our formidable posse comitatus. Sentinels were placed at the back and front of the house the moment we got to it; a tremendous battery of knocks was directed against the door; a light appeared at a window; I was told to conceal myself behind the police; then came more knocks and a cry of "Open in the name of the law!" At that terrible summons bolts and locks gave way before an invisible hand, and the moment after the subprefect was in the passage, confronting a waiter half dressed and ghastly pale. This was the short dialogue which immediately took place:

"We want to see the Englishman who is sleeping in this house."

"He went away hours ago."

"He did no such thing. His friend went away; he remained. Show us to his bedroom!"

"I swear to you, Monsieur le Sous-prefet, he is not here! he - "

"I swear to you, Monsieur le Garcon, he is. He slept here; he didn't find your bed comfortable; he came to us to complain of it; here he is among my men; and here am I ready to look for a flea or two in his bedstead. Renaudin!" (calling to one of the subordinates, and pointing to the waiter), "collar that man, and tie his hands behind him. Now then, gentlemen, let us walk upstairs!"

Every man and woman in the house was secured - the "old soldier" the first. Then I identified the bed in which I had slept, and then we went into the room above.

No object that was at all extraordinary appeared in any part of it. The subprefect looked round the place, commanded everybody to be silent, stamped twice on the floor, called for a candle, looked attentively at the spot he had stamped on, and ordered the flooring there to be carefully taken up. This was done in no time. Lights were produced, and we saw a deep raftered cavity between the floor of this room and the ceiling of the room beneath. Through this cavity there ran perpendicularly a sort of case of iron, thickly greased; and inside the case appeared the screw, which communicated with the bedtop below. Extra lengths of screw, freshly oiled; levers covered with felt; all the complete upper works of a heavy press - constructed with infernal ingenuity so as to join the fixtures below, and when taken to pieces again to go into the smallest possible compass - were next discovered and pulled out on the floor. After some little difficulty the subprefect succeeded in putting the machinery together, and, leaving his men to work it, descended with me to the bedroom. The smothering canopy was then lowered, but not so noiselessly as I had seen it lowered. When I mentioned this to the subprefect, his answer, simple as it was, had a terrible significance. "My men," said he, "are working down the bedtop for the first time; the men whose money you won were in better practice."

We left the house in the sole possession of two police agents, every one of the inmates being removed to prison on the spot. The subprefect, after taking down my proces verbal in his office, returned with me to my hotel to get my passport. "Do you think," I asked, as I gave it to him, "that any men have really been smothered in that bed, as they tried to smother me?"

"I have seen dozens of drowned men laid out at the morgue," answered the subprefect, "in whose pocket-books were found letters stating that they had committed suicide in the Seine, because they had lost everything at the gaming-table. Do I know how many of those men entered the same gambling-house that you entered? won as you won? took that bed as you took it? slept in it? were smothered in it? and were privately thrown into the river, with a letter of explanation written by the murderers and placed in their pocket-books? No man can say how many or how few have suffered the fate from which you have escaped. The people of the gambling-house kept their bedstead machinery a secret from us - even from the police! The dead kept the rest of the secret for them. Good-night, or rather good-morning, Monsieur Faulkner! Be at my office again at nine o'clock; in the meantime, au revoir !"

The rest of my story is soon told. I was examined and reexamined; the gambling-house was strictly searched all through from top to bottom; the prisoners were separately interrogated, and two of the less guilty among them made a confession. I discovered that the old soldier was master of the gambling-house - justice discovered that he had been drummed out of the army as a vagabond years ago; that he had been guilty of all sorts of villainies since; that he was in possession of stolen property, which the owners identified; and that he, the croupier, another accomplice, and the woman who had made my cup of coffee were all in the secret of the bedstead. There appeared some reason to doubt whether the inferior persons attached to the house knew anything of the suffocating machinery; and they received the benefit of that doubt, by being treated simply as thieves and vagabonds. As for the old soldier and his two head myrmidons, they went to the galleys; the woman who had drugged my coffee was imprisoned for I forget how many years; the regular attendants at the gambling-house were considered "suspicious," and placed under "surveillance"; and I became, for one whole week (which is a long time), the head "lion" in Parisian society. My adventure was dramatised by three illustrious play-makers, but never saw theatrical daylight; for the censorship forbade the introduction on the stage of a correct copy of the gambling-house bedstead.

One good result was produced by my adventure, which any censorship must have approved: it cured me of ever again trying rouge-et-noir as an amusement. The sight of a green cloth, with packs of cards and heaps of money on it, will henceforth be for ever associated in my mind with the sight of a bed canopy descending to suffocate me in the silence and darkness of the night.

Just as Mr. Faulkner pronounced these words he started in his chair, and resumed his stiff, dignified position in a great hurry. "Bless my soul!" cried he, with a comic look of astonishment and vexation, "while I have been telling you what is the real secret of my interest in the sketch you have so kindly given to me, I have altogether forgotten that I came here to sit for my portrait. For the last hour or more I must have been the worst model you ever had to draw from!"

"On the contrary, you have been the best," said I. "I have been trying to catch your likeness; and, while telling your story, you have unconsciously shown me the natural expression I wanted to insure my success."

NOTE BY MRS. KERBY

I cannot let this story end without mentioning what the chance saying was which caused it to be told at the farmhouse the other night. Our friend the young sailor, among his other quaint objections to sleeping on shore, declared that he particularly hated four-post beds, because he never slept in one without doubting whether the top might not come down in the night and suffocate him. I thought this chance reference to the distinguishing feature of William's narrative curious enough, and my husband agreed with me. But he says it is scarcely worth while to mention such a trifle in anything so important as a book. I cannot venture, after this, to do more than slip these lines in modestly at the end of the story. If the printer should notice my few last words, perhaps he may not mind the trouble of putting them into some out-of-the-way corner, in very small type.

L. K.

MICHEL LORIO'S CROSS

In the southwest point of Normandy, separated from Brittany only by a narrow and straight river, like the formal canals of Holland, stands the curious granite rock which is called Mont St. Michel. It is an isolated peak, rising abruptly out of a vast plain of sand to the height of nearly four hundred feet, and so precipitous toward the west that scarcely a root of grass finds soil enough in its weather-beaten clefts. At the very summit is built that wonderful church, the rich architecture and flying buttresses of which strike the eye leagues and leagues away, either on the sea or the mainland. Below the church, and supporting it by a solid masonry, is a vast pile formerly a fortress, castle, and prison; with caverns and dungeons hewn out of the living rock, and vaulted halls and solemn crypts; all desolate and solitary now, except when a party of pilgrims or tourists pass through them, ushered by a guide. Still lower down the rock, along its eastern and southern face, there winds a dark and narrow street, with odd, antique houses on either side. The only conveyance that can pass along it is the water-cart which supplies the town with fresh water from the mainland. The whole place is guarded by a strong and high rampart, with bastions and battlemented walls; and the only entrance is through three gateways, one immediately behind the other, with a small court between. The second of these strong gateways is protected by two old cannon, taken from the English in 1423, and still pointed out to visitors with inextinguishable pride by the natives of Mont. St. Michel.

A great plain of sand stretches around the Mont for miles every way - of sand or sea, for the water covers it at flood-tides, beating up against the foot of the granite rocks and the granite walls of the ramparts. But at neap tides and eaux mortes, as the French say, there is nothing but a desert of brown, bare sand, with ripple-marks lying across it, and with shallow, ankle-deep pools of salt water here and there. Afar off on the western sky-line a silver fringe of foam, glistening in the sunshine, marks the distant boundary to which the sea has retreated. On every other side of the horizon rises a belt of low cliffs, bending into a semicircle, with sweeping outlines of curves miles in length, drawn distinctly against the clear sky.

The only way to approach the Mont is across the sands. Each time the tide recedes a fresh track must be made, like the track along snowy roads; and every traveller, whether on foot or in carriage, must direct his steps by this scarcely beaten path. Now and then he passes a high, strong post, placed where there is any dangerous spot upon the plain; for there are perilous quicksands, imperceptible to any eye, lurking in sullen and patient treachery for any unwary footstep. The river itself, which creeps sluggishly in a straight black line across the brown desert, has its banks marked out by rows of these high stakes, with a bush of leafless twigs at the top of each. A dreary, desolate, and barren scene it is, with no life in it except the isolated life upon the Mont.

This little family of human beings, separated from the great tide of life like one of the shallow pools which the ebbing sea has left upon its sands, numbers scarcely a hundred and a half. The men are fishers, for there is no other occupation to be followed on the sterile rock. Every day also the level sweep of sands is wandered over by the women and children, who seek for cockles in the little pools; the babble of whose voices echoes far through the quiet air, and whose shadows fall long and unbroken on the brown wilderness. Now and then the black-robed figure of a priest, or of one of the brothers dwelling in the monument on the top of the rock, may be seen slowly pacing along the same dead level, and skirting the quicksands where the warning posts are erected. In the summer months bands of pilgrims are also to be seen marching in a long file like travellers across the desert; but in winter these visits cease almost wholly, and the inhabitants of the Mont are left to themselves.

Having so little intercourse with the outer world, and living on a rock singled out by supernatural visitants, the people remain more superstitious than even the superstitious Germans and Bretons who are their neighbours. Few of them can read or write. The new thoughts, opinions, and creeds of the present century do not reach them. They are contented with the old faith, bound up for them in the history of their patron, the archangel St. Michel, and with the minute interest taken in every native of the rock. Each person knows the history of every other inhabitant, but knows little else.

From Pontorson to the Mont the road lies along the old Bay of St. Michel, with low hedge-rows of feathery tamarind-trees on each side as far as the beach. It is not at all a solitary road, for hundreds of long, heavy carts, resembling artillery waggons, encumber it, loaded with a gray shaly deposit dug out of the bay: a busy scene of men and women digging in the heavy sand, while the shaggy horses stand by, hanging their heads patiently under the blue-stained sheepskins about their necks.

Two or three persons are at work at every cart; one of them, often a woman, standing on the rising pile, and beating it flat with a spade, while a cheerful clatter of voices is heard on every hand.

But at one time a man might have been seen there working alone, quite alone. Even a space was left about him, as if an invisible circle were drawn, within which no person would venture. If a word were flung at him across this imaginary cordon, it was nothing but a taunt or a curse, and it was invariably spoken by a man. No woman so much as glanced at him. He toiled on doggedly, and in silence, with a weary-looking face, until his task was ended, and the waggon driven off by the owner, who had employed him at a lower rate than his comrades. Then he would throw his blue blouse over his shoulders, and tramp away with heavy tread along the faintly marked trail leading across the beach to Mont St. Michel.

Neither was there any voice to greet him as he gained the gateway, where the men of the Mont congregated, as they always congregate about the entrance to a walled town. Rather, the scornful silence which had surrounded him at his work was here deepened into a personal hatred. Within the gate the women, who were chattering over their nets of cockles, shrank away from him, or broke into a contemptuous laugh. Along the narrow street the children fled at the sight of him, and hid behind their mothers, from whose protection they could shout after him. If the cure met him, he would turn aside into the first house rather than come in contact with him. He was under a ban which no one dared to defy.

The only voice that spoke to him was the fretful, querulous voice of an old, bedridden woman as he lifted the latch and opened the door of a poor house upon the ramparts, which had no entrance into the street; and where he lived alone with his mother, cut off from all accidental intercourse with his neighbours.

"Michel! Michel! how late thou art!" she exclaimed; "if thou hadst been a good son thou wouldst have returned before the hour it is."

"I returned as soon as my work was finished," he answered, in a patient voice; "I have not lost a minute by the way."

"Bah! because no one will ask thee to turn in with them anywhere!" she continued. "If thou wert like everybody else thou wouldst have many a friend to pass thy time with. It is hard for me, thy mother, to have brought thee into the world that all the world should despise and hate thee, as they do this day. Monsieur le Cure says there is no hope for thee if thou art so obstinate; thou must go to hell, though I named thee after our great archangel St. Michel, and brought thee up as a good Christian. Quel malheur! How hard it is for me to lie in bed all day, and think of my son in the flames of hell!"

Very quietly, as if he had heard such complainings hundreds of times before, did Michel set about kindling a few sticks upon the open hearth. This was so common a welcome home that he scarcely heard it, and had ceased to heed it. The room, as the flickering light fell upon it, was one of the cheerless and comfortless chambers to be seen in any peasant's house: a pile of wood in one corner, a single table with a chair or two, a shelf with a few pieces of brown crockery, and the bed on which the paralytic woman was lying, her hands crossed over her breast, and her bright black eyes glistening in the gloom. Michel brought her the soup he had made, and fed her carefully and tenderly, before thinking of satisfying his own hunger.

"It is of no good, Michel," she said, when he laid her down again upon the pillow he had made smooth for her; "it is of no good. Thou mayest as well leave me to perish; it will not weigh for thee. Monsieur le Cure says if thou hadst been born a heretic perhaps the good God might have taken it into account. But thou wert born a Christian, as good a Christian as all the world, and thou hast sold thy birthright to the devil. Leave me then, and take thy pleasure in this life, for thou wilt have nothing but misery in the next."

"I will not leave thee - never!" he answered, briefly. "I have no fear of the next world."

He was a man of few words evidently. Perhaps the silence maintained around him had partly frozen his power of speech. Even to his mother he spoke but little, though her complaining went on without ceasing, until he extinguished both fire and lamp, and climbed the rude ladder into the loft overhead, where her voice never failed to rouse him from his sleep, if she only called "Michel!" He could not clearly explain his position even to himself. He had gone to Paris many years before, where he came across some Protestants, who had taught him to read the Testament, and instructed him in their religion. The new faith had taken hold of him, and thrust deep roots into his simple and constant nature; though he had no words at command to express the change to others, and scarcely to himself. So long as he had been in Paris there had been no need of this.

But now his father's death had compelled him to return to his native place, and to the little knot of people who knew him as old Pierre Lorio's son, a fisherman like themselves, with no more right to read or think than they had. The fierceness of the persecution he encountered filled him with dismay, though it had not shaken his fidelity to his new faith. But often a dumb, inarticulate longing possessed him to make known to his old neighbours the reason of the change in him, but speech failed him. He could only stammer out his confession, "I am no longer a Catholic, I am a Protestant, I cannot pray to the saints, not even to the archangel St. Michel or the Blessed Virgin. I pray only to God." For anything else, for explanation, and for all argument, he had no more language than the mute, wistful language one sees in the eyes of dumb creatures, when they gaze fully at us.

Perhaps there is nothing more pitiful than the painful want of words to express that which lies deepest within us; a want common to us all, but greatest in those who have had no training in thus shaping and expressing their inmost thoughts.

There was not much to fear from a man like this. Michel Lorio was a living lesson against apostasy. As he went up and down the street, and in and out of the gate, his loneliness and dejection spoke more eloquently for the old faith than any banishment could have done. Michel was suffered to remain under a ban, not formal and ceremonial, but a tacit ban, which quite as effectively set him apart, and made his life more solitary than if he had been dwelling alone on a desert rock out at sea.

Michel accepted his lot without complaint and without bitterness. He never passed Monsieur le Cure without a salutation. When he went daily for water to the great cistern of the monastery, he was always ready to carry the brimful pails too heavy for the arms of the old women and children. If he had leisure he mounted the long flights of grass-grown steps three or four times for his neighbours, depositing his burden at their doors, without a word of thanks for his help being vouchsafed to him. Now and then he overheard a sneer at his usefulness; and his mother taunted him often for his patience and forbearance. But he went on his way silently with deeper yearning for human love and sympathy than he could make known.

If it had not been that, when he was kneeling at the rude dormer-window of his loft and gazing dreamily across the wide sweep of sand, with the moon shining across it and the solemn stars lighting up the sky, he was at times vaguely conscious of an influence, almost a presence, as of a hand that touched him and a voice that spoke to him, he must have sunk under this intense longing for love and fellowship. Had he been a Catholic still, he would have believed that the archangel St. Michel was near and about to manifest himself as in former times in his splendid shrine upon the Mont. The new faith had not cast out all the old superstitious nature; yet it was this vague spiritual presence which supported him under the crushing and unnatural conditions of his social life. He endured, as seeing one who is invisible.

Yet at other times he could not keep his feet away from the little street where all the life there was might be found. At night he would creep cautiously along the ramparts and descend by a quiet staircase into an angle of the walls, where he could look on unseen upon the gathering of townsfolk in the inn where he had often gone with his father in earlier days. The landlord, Nicolas, was a most bitter enemy now. There was the familiar room filled with bright light from an oil-lamp and the brighter flicker of a wood fire where the landlord's wife was cooking. A deep, low recess in the corner, with a crimson valance stretched across it, held a bed with snow-white pillows, upon one of which rested a child's curly head with eyes fast sealed against the glare of the lamp. At a table close by sat the landlord and three or four of the wealthier men of the Mont busily and seriously eating the omelets and fried fish served to them from the pan over the fire.

The copper and brass cooking utensils glittered in the light from the walls where they hung. It was a cheery scene, and Michel would stand in his cold, dark corner, watching it until all was over and the guests ready to depart.

"Thou art Michel le diable!" said a childish voice to him one evening, and he felt a small, warm hand laid for an instant upon his own. It was Delphine, Nicolas's eldest girl, a daring child, full of spirit and courage; yet even she shrank back a step or two after touching him, and stood as if ready to take flight.

"I am Michel Lorio," he answered, in a quiet, pleasant voice, which won her back to his side. "Why dost thou call me Michel le diable?"

"All the world calls thee that," answered Delphine; "thou art a heretic. See, I am a good Christian. I say my ave and paternoster every night; if thou wilt do the same thing, no one will call thee Michel le diable."

"Thou art not afraid of me?" he asked, for the child put her hand again on his.

"No, no! thou art not the real devil!" she said, "and maman has put my name on the register of the monument; so the great archangel St. Michel will deliver me from all evil. What canst thou do? Canst thou turn children into cats? or canst thou walk across the sea without being drowned? or canst thou stand on the highest pinnacle of the church, where the golden image of St. Michel used to be, and cast thyself down without killing thyself? I will go back with thee to thy house and see what thou canst do."

"I can do none of these things," answered Michel, "not one; but thou shalt come home with me if thou wilt."

"Carry me," she said, "that I may feel how strong thou art."

He lifted her easily into his arms, for he was strong and accustomed to bear heavier burdens. His heart beat fast as the child's hand stole round his neck and her soft cheek touched his own. Delphine had never been upon the ramparts before when the stars were out and the distant circle of the cliffs hidden by the night, and several times he was compelled to stop and answer her eager questions; but she would not go into the house when they reached the door.

"Carry me back again, Michel," she demanded. "I do not like thy mother. Thou shalt bring me again along the ramparts to-morrow night. I will always come to thee, always when I see thee standing in the dark corner by our house. I love thee much, Michel le diable."

It was a strange friendship carried on stealthily. Michel could not put away from himself this one little tie of human love and fellowship. As for Delphine, she was as silent about her new friend as children often are of such things which affect them deeply. There was a mingling of superstitious feeling in her affection for Michel - a half-dread that gave their secret meetings a greater charm to the daring spirit of the child. The evening was a busy time at the inn, and if Delphine had been missed, but little wonder and no anxiety would have been aroused at her absence. The ramparts were deserted after dark, and no one guessed that the two dark figures sauntering to and fro were Michel and Delphine. When the nights were too cold they took refuge in a little overhanging turret projecting from one of the angles of the massive walls - a darksome niche with nothing but the sky to be seen through a narrow embrasure in the shape of a cross. In these haunts Michel talked in his simple untaught way of his thoughts and of his new faith, pouring into the child's ear what he could never tell to any other. By day Delphine never seemed to see him; never cast a look toward him as he passed by amid the undisguised ill will of the town. She ceased to speak of him even, with the unconscious and natural dissimulation by which children screen themselves from criticism and censure.

The people of the Mont St. Michel are very poor, and the women and children are compelled to seek some means of earning money as well as the men. As long as the summer lasts the crowds of pilgrims and tourists, flocking to the wonderful fortress and shrine upon the summit, bring employment and gain to some portion of them; but in the winter there is little to do except when the weather is fine enough to search for shell-fish about the sands, and sell them in the villages of the mainland. As the tide goes down, bands of women and children follow it out for miles, taking care to retrace their steps before the sea rises again. From Michel's cottage on the ramparts the whole plain toward Avranches was visible, and he could hear the busy hum of voices coming to his ear from afar through the quiet air. But on the western side of the Mont, where the black line of the river crosses the sands, they are more dangerous; and in this direction only the more venturesome seekers go - boys who love any risk, and widows who are the more anxious to fill their nets because they have no man to help them in getting their daily bread.

The early part of the winter is not cold in Normandy, especially by the sea. As long as the westerly winds sweep across the Atlantic, the air is soft though damp, with fine mists hanging in it, which shine with rainbow tints in the sunlight. Sometimes Christmas and the New Year find the air still genial, in spite of the short days and the long rainy nights. Strong gales may blow, but so long as they do not come from the dry east or frosty north there is no real severity of weather.

It was such a Christmas week that year. Not one of the women or children had yet been forced to stay away from the sands on account of the cold. Upon Christmas eve there was a good day, though, a short one, before them, for it was low water about noon, and the high tide would not be in before six. All the daylight would be theirs. It was a chance not to be missed, for as the tides grew later in the day their time for fishing would be cut shorter. Almost every woman and child turned out through the gate with their nets in their hands. By midday the plain was dotted over by them, and the wintry sun shone pleasantly down, and the quiet rock caught the echo of their voices. Farther away, out of sight and hearing, the men also were busy, Michel among them, casting nets upon the sea. As the low sun went down in the southern sky, the scattered groups came home by twos and threes, anxious to bring in their day's fishing in time for the men to carry them across to the mainland before the Mont should be shut in by the tide.

A busy scene was that in the gateway.

All the town was there; some coming in from the sands, and those who had been left at home with babies or old folks running down from their houses. There was chaffing and bartering; exchanges agreed upon, and commissions innumerable to be intrusted to the men about to set out for Pontorson, the nearest town. Michel Lorio was going to sell his own fish, for who would carry it for him? Yet though he was the first who was ready to start, not a soul charged him with a single commission. He lingered wistfully and loitered just outside the gateway; but neither man, woman, nor child said, "Michel, bring me what I want from the town."

He was treading slowly down the rough causeway under the walls of the town, when a woman's shrill voice startled him. It was not far from sunset, and the sun was sinking round and red behind a bank of fog. A thin gray mist was creeping up from the sea. The latest band of stragglers, a cluster of mere children, were running across the sand to the gate. Michel turned round and saw Nicolas's wife, a dark, stern-looking woman, beckoning vehemently to these children. He paused for a moment to look at his little Delphine. "Not there!" he said to himself, and was passing on, when the shrill voice again caught his attention.

"Where is Phine?" called the mother.

What was it the children said? What answer had they shouted back? Michel stood motionless, as if all strength had failed him suddenly. The children rushed past him in a troop. He lifted up his eyes, looking fearfully toward the sea hidden behind the deepening fog. Was it possible that he had heard them say that Delphine was lost?

"Where is Phine?" asked the mother; but though her voice was lower now, Michel heard every syllable loudly. It seemed as if he could have heard a whisper, though the chattering in the gateway was like the clamour of a fair. The eldest girl in the little band spoke in a hurried and frightened tone.

"Phine is so naughty, madame," she said, "we could not keep her near us. She would go on and on to the sea. We could not wait for her. We heard her calling, but it was so far, we dared not go back. But she cannot be far behind us, for we shouted as we came along. She will be here soon, madame."

"Mon Dieu!" cried the mother, sinking down on one of the great stones, either rolled up by the tide, or left by the masons who built the ramparts. "Call her father to me."

It was Michel Lorio who found Nicolas, his greatest enemy. Nicolas had a number of errands to be done in the town, and he was busy impressing them on the memory of his messenger, who, like every one else, could neither read nor write. When Michel caught his arm in a sharp, fast grip, he turned round with a scowl, and tried, but in vain, to shake off his grasp.

"Come to thy wife," said Michel, dragging him toward the gate; "Delphine, thy little one, is lost on the sands."

The whole crowd heard the words, for Michel's voice was pitched in a high, shrill key, which rang above the clamour and the babel. There was an instant hush, every one listening to Michel, and every eye fastened upon him. Nicolas stared blankly at him, as if unable to understand him, yet growing passive under his sense of bewilderment.

"The children who went out with Delphine this morning are come back," continued Michel, in the same forced tone; "they are come back without her. She is lost on the sands. The night is falling, and there is a fog. I tell you the little one is alone, quite alone, upon the sands; and it will be high water at six o'clock. Delphine is alone and lost upon the sands!"

The momentary hush of the crowd was at an end. The children began crying, and the women calling loudly upon St. Michel and the Holy Virgin. The men gathered about Nicolas and Michel, and went down in a compact group to the causeway beyond the gate. There the lurid sun, shining dimly through the fog, made the most sanguine look grave and shake their heads hopelessly behind the father and mother. The latter sat motionless, looking out with straining eyes to see if Delphine were not coming through the thickening mist.

"Mais que faire! que faire!" cried Nicolas, catching at somebody's shoulder for support without seeing whose it was. It was Michel's, who had not stirred from his side since he had first clasped his arm. Michel's face was as white as the mother's; but there was a resolute light in his eyes that was not to be seen in hers.

"Nothing can be done," answered one of the oldest men in answer to Nicolas's cry, "nothing, nothing! We do not know where the child is lost. See! there are leagues and leagues of sand; and one might wander miles away from where the poor little creature is at this instant. The great archangel St. Michel protect her!"

"I will go," said the mother, lifting herself up; and, raising her voice, she called loudly, with a cry that rang and echoed against the walls, "Phine! Phine! my little Phine, come back to thy poor mother!" But there was no answer, except the sobs and prayers of the women and children clustering behind her.

"Thou canst not go!" exclaimed Nicolas; "there are our other little ones to think of; nor can I leave thee and them. My God! is there then no one who will go and seek my little Delphine?"

"I will go," answered Michel, standing out from among the crowd, and facing it with his white face and resolute eyes; "there is only one among you all upon the Mont who will miss me. I leave my mother to your care. There is no time for me to bid her adieu. If I come back alive, well! if I perish, that will be well also!"

Even then there was no cordiality of response on the hearts of his old friends and neighbours. The superstition and prejudice of long years could not be broken down in one moment and by one act of self-sacrifice. They watched Michel as he laid his full creel down from his shoulders, and threw across them the strong square net with which he fished in the ebbing tide. His silence was no less expressive than theirs. Without a sound he passed away barefooted down the rude causeway. His face, as the sun shone on it, was set and resolute with a determination to face the end, whatever the end might be. He might have so trodden the path to Calvary.

He longed to speak to them, to say adieu to them; but he waited in vain for one voice to break the silence. He turned round before he was too far away, and saw them still clustered without the gate; every one of them known to him from his boyhood, the story of whose lives had been bound up with his own and formed a part of his history. They were all there, except his mother, who would soon hear what peril of the sea and peril of the night he was about to face. Tears dimmed his eyes, and made the group grow indistinct, as though the mist had already gathered between him and them. Then he quickened his steps, and the people of Mont St. Michel lost sight of him behind a great buttress of the ramparts.

But for a time Michel could still see the Mont as he hurried along its base, going westward, where the most treacherous sands lie. His home was on the eastern side, and he could see nothing of it. But the great rock rose up precipitously above him, and the noble architecture upon its highest point glowed with a ruddy tint in the setting light. As he trampled along no sound could be heard but the distant sigh of the sea, and the low, sad sough of the sand as his bare feet trod it. The fog before him was not dense, only a light haze, deceptive and beguiling; for here and there he turned aside, fancying he could see Delphine, but as he drew nearer to the spot he discovered nothing but a post driven into the sand. There was no fear that he should lose himself upon the bewildering level, for he knew his way as well as if the sand had been laid out in well-defined tracks. His dread was lest he should not find Delphine soon enough to escape from the tide, which would surely overwhelm them both.

He scarcely knew how the time sped by, but the sun had sunk below the horizon, and he had quite lost the Mont in the fog. The brown sand and the gray dank mist were all that he could see, yet still he plodded on westward, toward the sea, calling into the growing darkness. At last he caught the sound of a child's sobs and crying, which ceased for a moment when he turned in that direction and shouted, "Phine!" Calling to one another, it was not long before he saw the child wandering forlornly and desolately in the mist. She ran sobbing into his open arms, and Michel lifted her up and held her to his heart with a strange rapture.

"It is thou that hast found me," she said, clinging closely to him. "Carry me back to my mother. I am safe now, quite safe. Did the archangel St. Michel send thee?"

There was not a moment to be lost; Michel knew that

full well. The moan of the sea was growing louder every minute, though he could not see its advancing line. There was no spot upon the sand that would not be covered before another hour was gone, and there was barely time, if enough, to get back to the Mont. He could not waste time or breath in talking to the child he held fast in his arms. A pale gleam of moonlight shone through the vapour, but of little use to him save to throw a ghostly glimmer across the sands. He strode hurriedly along, breathing hardly through his teeth and clasping Delphine so fast that she grew frightened at his silence and haste.

"Where art thou taking me, Michel le diable?" she said, beginning to struggle in his arms. "Let me down; let me down, I tell thee! Maman has said I must never look at thee. Thou shalt not carry me any farther."

There was strength enough in the child and her vehement struggles to free herself to hinder Michel in his desperate haste. He was obliged to stand still for a minute or two to pacify her, speaking in his quiet, patient voice, which she knew so well.

"Be tranquil, my little Phine," he said. "I am come to save thee. As the Lord Jesus came to seek and to save those who are lost, so am I come to seek thee and carry thee back to thy mother. It is dark here, my child, and the sea is rising quickly, quickly. But thou shalt be safe. Be tranquil, and let me make haste back to the Mont."

"Did the Lord save thee in this manner?" asked Delphine, eagerly.

"Yes, He saved me like this," answered Michel. "He

laid down His life for mine. Now thou must let me save thee."

"I will be good and wise," said the child, putting her arms again about his neck, while he strode on, striving if possible to regain the few moments that had been lost. But it was not possible. He knew that before he had gone another kilometre, when through the mist there rose before him the dark, colossal form of the Mont, but too far away still for them both to reach it in safety. Thirty minutes were essential for him to reach the gates with his burden, but in little more than twenty the sea would be dashing round the walls. The tide was yet out of sight and the sands were dry, but it would rush in before many minutes, and the swiftest runner with no weight to carry could not outrun it. Both could not be saved; could either of them? He had foreseen this danger and provided for it.

"My little Phine," he said, "thou wilt not be afraid if I place thee where thou wilt be quite safe from the sea? See, here is my net! I will put thee within it, and hang it on one of these strong stakes, and I will stand below thee. Thou wilt be brave and good. Let us be quick, very quick. It will be like a swing for thee, and thou wilt not be afraid so long as I stand below thee."

Even while he spoke he was busy fastening the corners of his net securely over the stake, hanging it above the reach of the last tide-mark. Delphine watched him laughing. It seemed only another pleasant adventure, like wandering with him upon the ramparts, or taking shelter in the turret. The net held her comfortably, and by stooping down she could touch with her outstretched hand the head of Michel. He stood below her, his arms fast locked about the stake, and his face uplifted to her in the faint light.

"Phine," he said, "thou must not be afraid when the water lies below thee, even if I do not speak. Thou art safe."

"Art thou safe also, Michel?" she asked.

"Yes, I am quite safe also," he answered; "but I shall be very quiet. I shall not speak to thee. Yes; the Lord Christ is caring for me, as I for thee. He bound Himself to the cross as I bind myself here. This is my cross, Delphine. I understand it better now. He loved us and gave Himself for us. Tell them to-morrow what I say to thee. I am as safe as thou art, tranquil and happy."

"We shall not be drowned!" said Delphine, half in confidence and half in dread of the sea, which was surging louder and louder through the darkness.

"Not thou!" he answered, cheerily. "But, Phine, tell them to-morrow that I shall nevermore be solitary and sad. I leave thee now, and then I shall be with Christ. I wish I could have spoken to them, but my heart and tongue were heavy. Hark! there is the bell ringing."

The bell which is tolled at night, when travellers are crossing the sands, to guide them to the Mont, flung its clear, sharp notes down from the great indistinct rock, looming through the dusk.

"It is like a voice to me, the voice of a friend; but it is too late!" murmured Michel. "Art thou happy, Delphine, my little one? When I cease to speak to thee wilt thou not be afraid? I shall be asleep, perhaps. Say thy paternoster now, for it is growing late with me."

The bell was still toiling, but with a quick, hurried movement, as if those who rang it were fevered with impatience. The roaring of the tide, as it now poured in rapidly over the plain, almost drowned its clang.

"Touch me with thy little hand, touch me quickly!" cried Michel. "Remember to tell them to-morrow that I loved them all always, and I would have given myself for them as I do for thee. Adieu, my little Phine. Come quickly, Lord Jesus!"

The child told afterward that the water rose so fast that she dared not look at it, but shut her eyes as it spread, white and shimmering, in the moonlight all around her. She began to repeat her paternoster, but she forgot how the words came. But she heard Michel, in a loud clear voice, saying "Our Father"; only he also seemed to forget the words, for he did not say more than "Forgive us our trespasses, as we forgive - ." Then he became quite silent, and when she spoke to him, after a long while, he did not answer her. She supposed he had fallen asleep, as he had said, but she could not help crying and calling to him again and again. The sea-gulls flew past her screaming, but there was no sound of any voice to speak to her. In spite of what he had said to her beforehand she grew frightened, and thought it was because she had been unkind to Michel le diable that she was left there alone, with the sea swirling to and fro beneath her.

It was not for more than two or three hours that Delphine hung cradled in Michel's net, for the tide does not lie long round the Mont St. Michel, and flows out again as swiftly as it comes in. The people followed it out, scattering over the sands in the forlorn hope of finding the dead bodies of Michel Lorio and the child, for they had no expectation of meeting with either of them alive. At last two or three of them heard the voice of Delphine, who saw the glimmer of their lanterns upon the sands, and called shrilly and loudly for succour.

They found her swinging safely in her net, untouched by the water. But Michel had sunk down upon his knees, though his arms were still fastened about the stake. His head had fallen forward upon his breast, and his thick wet hair covered his face. They lifted him without a word spoken. He had saved Delphine's life at the cost of his own.

All the townspeople were down at the gate, waiting for the return of those who had gone out to seek for the dead. The moon had risen above the fog, and shone clearly down upon them. Delphine's mother, with her younger children about her, sat on the stone where she had been sitting when Michel set out on his perilous quest. She and the other women could see a crowd of the men coming back, carrying some burden among them. But as they drew near to the gate, Delphine sprang forward from among them and ran and threw herself into her mother's arms. "A miracle!" cried some voices amid the crowd; a miracle wrought by their patron St. Michel. If Michel Lorio were safe, surely he would become again a good Christian, and return to his ancient faith. But Michel Lorio was dead, and all that could be done for him was to carry his dead body home to his paralytic mother, and lay it upon his bed in the little loft where he had spent so many hours of sorrowful loneliness.

It was a perplexing problem to the simple people. Some said that Michel had been permitted to save the child by a diabolic agency which had failed him when he sought to save himself. Others maintained that it was no other than the great archangel St. Michel who had securely fastened the net upon the stake and so preserved Delphine, while the heretic was left to perish. A few thought secretly, and whispered it in fear, that Michel had done a noble deed, and won heaven thereby. The cure, who came to look upon the calm dead face, opened his lips after long and profound thought:

"If this man had been a Christian," he said, "he would have been a saint and a martyr."

A PERILOUS AMOUR

AN EPISODE ADAPTED FROM THE MEMOIRS
OF
MAXIMILIAN DE BETHUNE, DUKE OF SULLY

Such in brief were the reasons which would have led me, had I followed the promptings of my own sagacity, to oppose the return of the Jesuits. It remains for me only to add that these arguments lost all their weight when set in the balance against the safety of my beloved master. To this plea the king himself for once condescended, and found those who were most strenuous to dissuade him the least able to refute it; since the more a man abhorred the Jesuits, the more ready he was to allow that the king's life could not be safe from their practices while the edict against them remained in force. The support which I gave to the king on this occasion exposed me to the utmost odium of my co-religionists, and was in later times ill-requited by the order. But a remarkable incident that occurred while the matter was still under debate, and which I now for the first time make public, proved beyond question the wisdom of my conduct.

Fontainebleau being at this time in the hands of the builders, the king had gone to spend his Easter at Chantilly, whither Mademoiselle d'Entragues had also repaired. During his absence from Paris I was seated one morning in my library at the Arsenal, when I was informed that Father Cotton, the same who at Metz had presented a petition from the Jesuits, and who was now in Paris pursuing that business under a safe-conduct, craved leave to pay his respects to me. I was not surprised, for I had been a little before this of some service to him. The pages of the court, while loitering outside the Louvre, had raised a tumult in the streets, and grievously insulted the father by shouting after him, "Old Wool! Old Cotton!" in imitation of the Paris street cry. For this the king, at my instigation, had caused them to be soundly whipped, and I supposed that the Jesuit now desired to thank me for advice - given, in truth, rather out of regard to discipline than to him. So I bade them admit him.

His first words, uttered before my secretaries could retire, indicated that this was indeed his errand; and for a few moments I listened to such statements from him and made such answers myself as became our several positions. Then, as he did not go, I began to conceive the notion that he had come with a further purpose; and his manner, which seemed on this occasion to lack ease, though he was well gifted with skill and address, confirmed the notion. I waited, therefore, with patience, and presently he named his Majesty with many expressions of devotion to his person. "I trust," said he, "that the air of Fontainebleau agrees with him, M. de Rosny?"

"You mean, good father, of Chantilly?" I answered.

"Ah, to be sure!" he rejoined, hastily. "He is, of course, at Chantilly."

After that he rose to depart, but was delayed by the raptures into which he fell at sight of the fire, which, the weather being cold for the time of year, I had caused to be lit. "It burns so brightly," said he, "that it must be of boxwood, M. de Rosny."

"Of boxwood?" I exclaimed, in surprise.

"Ay, is it not of boxwood?" quoth he, looking at me with much simplicity.

"Certainly not!" I made answer, rather peevishly. "Who ever heard of people burning boxwood in Paris, father?"

He apologised for his ignorance - which was indeed matter of wonder - on the ground of his southern birth, and took his departure, leaving me in much doubt as to the real purport of his visit. I was indeed more troubled by the uncertainty I felt than another less conversant with the methods of the Jesuits might have been, for I knew that it was their habit to let drop a word where they dared not speak plainly, and I felt myself put on my mettle to interpret the father's hint. My perplexities were increased by the belief that he would not have intervened in any matter of small moment, and by the conviction, which grew upon me apace, that while I stood idle before the hearth my dearest interests and those of France were at stake.

"Michel," I said at last, addressing the doyen of my secretaries, who chanced to be a Provencal, "have you ever seen a boxwood fire?"

He replied respectfully, but with some show of surprise, that he had not, adding that that wood was rendered so valuable to the turner by its hardness that few people would be extravagant enough to use it for fuel. I assented, and felt the more certain that the Jesuit's remark contained a hidden meaning. The only other clue I had consisted in the apparent mistake the father had made as to the king's residence, and this might have been dropped from him in pure inadvertence. Yet I was inclined to think it intentional, and construed it as implying that the matter concerned the king personally. Which the more alarmed me.

I passed the day in great anxiety, but toward evening, acting on a sudden inspiration, I sent La Trape, my valet, a trusty fellow who had saved my life at Cahors, to the Three Pigeons, a large inn in the suburbs, at which such travellers from North to South as did not wish to enter the city were accustomed to change horses and sometimes to sleep. Acquitting himself of the commission I had given him with his usual adroitness, he quickly returned with the news that a traveller of rank had passed through three days before, having sent in advance to order relays there and at Essonnes. La Trape reported that the gentleman had remained in his coach, and that none of the inn servants had seen his face.

"And he had companions?" I said. My mind had not failed already to conceive a natural suspicion.

"Only one, your Grace. The rest were servants."

"And that one?"

"A man in the yard fancied that he recognised M. de la Varenne."

"Ah!" I said no more. My agitation was indeed such that, before giving reins to it, I bade La Trape withdraw. I could scarcely believe that, perfectly acquainted as the king was with the plots which Spain and the Catholics were daily weaving for his life, and possessing such unavowed but powerful enemies among the great lords as Tremouille and Bouillon, to say nothing of Mademoiselle d'Entragues's half-brother, the Count of Auvergne - I could hardly believe that with this knowledge his Majesty had been so foolhardy as to travel without guards or attendance to Fontainebleau. And yet I now felt an absolute certainty that this was the case. The presence of La Varenne also, the confidant of his intrigues, informed me of the cause of this wild journey, convincing me that his Majesty had given way to the sole weakness of his nature, and was bent on one of those adventures of gallantry which had been more becoming in the Prince of Bearn than in the king of France. Neither was I at a loss to guess the object of his pursuit. It had been lately whispered in the court that the king had seen and fallen in love with his mistress's younger sister, Susette d'Entragues, whose home at Malesherbes lay but three leagues from Fontainebleau, on the edge of the forest. This placed the king's imprudence in a stronger light, for he had scarcely in France a more dangerous enemy than her brother Auvergne; nor had the immense sums which he had settled on the elder sister satisfied the mean avarice or conciliated the brutish hostility of her father.

Apprised of all this, I saw that Father Cotton had desired to communicate it to me. But his motive I found it less easy to divine. It might have been a wish to balk this new passion through my interference, and at the same time to expose me to the risk of his Majesty's anger. Or it might simply have been a desire to avert danger from the king's person. At any rate, constant to my rule of ever preferring my master's interest to his favour, I sent for Maignan, my equerry, and bade him have an equipage ready at dawn.

Accordingly at that hour next morning, attended only by La Trape, with a groom, a page, and four Swiss, I started, giving out that I was bound for Sully to inspect that demesne, which had formerly been the property of my family, and of which the refusal had just been offered to me. Under cover of this destination I was enabled to reach La Ferte Alais unsuspected. There, pretending that the motion of the coach fatigued me, I mounted the led horse, without which I never travelled, and bidding La Trape accompany me, gave orders to the others to follow at their leisure to Pethiviers, where I proposed to stay the night.

La Ferte Alais, on the borders of the forest, is some five leagues westward of Fontainebleau, and as far north of Malesherbes, with which last it is connected by a highroad. Having disclosed my intentions to La Trape, however, I presently left this road and struck into a path which promised to conduct us in the right direction. But the denseness of the undergrowth, and the huge piles of gray rocks which lie everywhere strewn about the forest, made it difficult to keep for any time in a straight line. After being two hours in the saddle we concluded that we had lost our way, and were confirmed in this on reaching a clearing, and seeing before us a small inn, which La Trape recognised as standing about a league and a half on the forest side of Malesherbes.

We still had ample time to reach Fontainebleau by nightfall, but before proceeding it was absolutely necessary that our horses should have rest.

Dismounting, therefore, I bade La Trape see the sorrel well baited. Observing that the inn was a poor place, and no one coming to wait upon me, I entered it of my own motion, and found myself at once in a large room better furnished with company than accommodation. Three men, who had the appearance of such reckless swaggering blades as are generally to be found drinking in the inns on the outskirts of Paris, and who come not unfrequently to their ends at Montfaucon, were tippling and playing cards at a table near the door. They looked up sullenly at my entrance, but refrained from saluting me, which, as I was plainly dressed and much stained by travel, was in some degree pardonable. By the fire, partaking of a coarse meal, was a fourth man of so singular an appearance that I must needs describe him. He was of great height and extreme leanness. His face matched his form, for it was long and thin, terminating in a small peaked beard which, like his hair and mustachios, was as white as snow. With all this, his eyes glowed with much of the fire of youth, and his brown complexion and sinewy hands seemed still to indicate robust health. He was dressed in garments which had once been fashionable, but now bore marks of long and rough usage, and I remarked that the point of his sword, which, as he sat, trailed on the stones behind him, had worn its way through the scabbard. Notwithstanding these signs of poverty, he saluted me with the ease and politeness of a gentleman, and bade me with much courtesy to share his table and the fire. Accordingly I drew up, and called for a bottle of the best wine, being minded to divert myself with him.

I was little prepared, however, for the turn his conversation took, and the furious tirade into which he presently broke, the object of which proved to be no other than myself! I do not know that I have ever cut so whimsical a figure as while hearing my name loaded with reproaches; but, being certain that he did not know me, I waited patiently, and soon learned both who he was, and the grievance which he was on his way to lay before the king. His name was Boisrose, and he had been the leader in that gallant capture of Fecamp, which took place while I was in Normandy as the king's representative. His grievance was that, notwithstanding promises in my letters, he had been deprived of the government of the place.

"He leads the king by the ear!" he declaimed loudly, in an accent which marked him for a Gascon. "That villain of a De Rosny! But I will show him up! I will trounce him!" With that he drew the hilt of his long rapier to the front with a gesture so truculent that the three bullies, who had stopped to laugh at him, resumed their game in disorder. Notwithstanding his hatred for me, I was pleased to meet with a man of so singular a temper, whom I also knew to be truly courageous; and I was willing to amuse myself further with him. "But," I said, modestly, "I have had some affairs with M. de Rosny, and I have never found him cheat me."

"Do not deceive yourself!" he roared, slapping the table. "He is a rascal!"

"Yet," I ventured to reply, "I have heard that in many respects he is not a bad minister."

"He is a villain!" he repeated, so loudly as to drown what I would have added. "Do not tell me otherwise. But rest assured! be happy, sir! I will make the king see him in his true colours! Rest content, sir! I will trounce him! He has to do with Armand de Boisrose!"

Seeing that he was not open to argument, - for, indeed, being opposed, he grew exceedingly warm, - I asked him by what channel he intended to approach the king, and learned that here he felt a difficulty, since he had neither a friend at court nor money to buy one. Being assured that he was an honest fellow, and knowing that the narrative of our rencontre and its sequel would vastly amuse his Majesty, who loved a jest of this kind, I advised Boisrose to go boldly to the king, which, thanking me as profusely as he had before reproached me, he agreed to do. With that I rose to depart.

At the last moment it occurred to me to try upon him the shibboleth which in Father Cotton's mouth had so mystified me.

"This fire burns brightly," I said, kicking the logs together with my riding-boot. "It must be of boxwood."

"Of what, sir?" quoth he, politely.

"Of boxwood, to be sure," I replied, in a louder tone.

"My certes!" he exclaimed. "They do not burn boxwood in this country. Those are larch trimmings - neither more nor less!"

While he wondered at my ignorance, I was pleased to discover his, and so far I had lost my pains. But it did not escape me that the three gamesters had ceased to play and were listening intently to our conversation. Moreover, as I moved to the door, they followed me with their eyes; and when I turned, after riding a hundred yards, I found that they had come to the door and were still gazing after us.

This prevented me at once remarking that a hound which had which had been lying before the fire had accompanied us, and was now running in front, now gambolling round us, as the manner of dogs is. When, however, after riding about two thirds of a league, we came to a place where the roads forked, I had occasion particularly to notice the hound, for, choosing one of the paths, it stood in the mouth of it, wagging its tail, and inviting us to take that road; and this so pertinaciously that, though the directions we had received at the inn would have led us to prefer the other, we determined to follow the dog as the more trustworthy guide.

We had proceeded about four hundred paces when La Trape pointed out that the path was growing more narrow and showed few signs of being used. So certain did it seem - though the dog still ran confidently ahead - that we were again astray, that I was about to draw rein and return, when I discovered with some emotion that the undergrowth on the right of the path had assumed the character of a thick hedge of box. Though less prone than most men to put faith in omens, I accepted this as one, and, notwithstanding that it wanted but an hour of sunset, I rode on steadily, remarking that, with each turn in the woodland path, the scrub on my left also gave place to the sturdy tree which had been in my mind all day. Finally we found ourselves passing through an alley of box, - which, no long time before, had been clipped and dressed, - until a final turn brought me into a cul-de-sac, a kind of arbor, carpeted with grass, and so thickly set about as to afford no exit save by the entrance. Here the dog placidly stood and wagged its tail, looking up at us.

I must confess that this termination of the adventure seemed so surprising, and the evening light shining on the walls of green round us was so full of a solemn quiet, that I was not surprised to hear La Trape mutter a short prayer. For my part, assured that something more than chance had brought me hither, I dismounted, and spoke encouragement to the hound; but it only leaped upon me. Then I walked round the enclosure, and presently remarked, close to the hedge, three small patches where the grass was slightly trodden down. Another glance told me much, for I saw that at these places the hedge, about three feet from the ground, bore traces of the axe. Choosing the nearest spot, I stooped, until my eyes were level with the hole thus made, and discovered that I was looking through a funnel skilfully cut in the wall of box. At my end the opening was rather larger than a man's face; at the other end about as large as the palm of the hand. The funnel rose gradually, so that I took the further extremity of it to be about seven feet from the ground, and here it disclosed a feather dangling on a spray. From the light falling strongly on this, I judged it to be not in the hedge, but a pace or two from it on the hither side of another fence of box. On examining the remaining loopholes I discovered that they bore upon the same feather.

My own mind was at once made up, but I bade my valet go through the same investigation, and then asked him whether he had ever seen an ambush of this kind laid for game. He replied at once that the shot would pass over the tallest stag; and, fortified by this, I mounted without saying more, and we retraced our steps. The hound presently slipped away, and without further adventure we reached Fontainebleau a little after sunset.

I expected to be received by the king with coldness and displeasure, but it chanced that a catarrh had kept him within doors all day, and, unable to hunt or to visit his new flame, he had been at leisure in this palace without a court to consider the imprudence he was committing. He received me, therefore, with the hearty laugh of a school-boy detected in a petty fault; and as I hastened to relate to him some of the things which M. de Boisrose had said of the Baron de Rosny, I soon had the gratification of perceiving that my presence was not taken amiss. His Majesty gave orders that bedding should be furnished for my pavilion, and that his household should wait on me, and himself sent me from his table a couple of chickens and a fine melon, bidding me at the same time to come to him when I had supped.

I did so, and found him alone in his closet, awaiting me with impatience, for he had already divined that I had not made this journey merely to reproach him. Before informing him, however, of my suspicions, I craved leave to ask him one or two questions, and, in particular, whether he had been in the habit of going to Malesherbes daily.

"Daily," he admitted, with a grimace. "What more, grand master?"

"By what road, sire?"

"I have commonly hunted in the morning and visited Malesherbes at midday. I have returned as a rule by the bridle-path, which crosses the Rock of the Serpents."

"Patience, sir, one moment," I said. "Does that path run anywhere through a plantation of box?"

"To be sure," he answered, without hesitation. "About half a mile on this side of the rock it skirts Madame Catherine's maze."

Thereon I told the king without reserve all that had happened. He listened with the air of apparent carelessness which he always assumed when the many plots against his life were under discussion; but at the end he embraced me again and again with tears in his eyes.

"France is beholden to you," he said. "I have never had, nor shall have, such another servant as you, Rosny! The three ruffians at the inn," he continued, "are the tools, of course, and the hound has been in the habit of accompanying them to the spot. Yesterday, I remember, I walked by that place with the bridle on my arm."

"By a special providence, sire," I said, gravely.

"It is true," he answered, crossing himself, a thing I had never yet known him to do in private. "But now, who is the craftsman who has contrived this pretty plot? Tell me that, grand master."

On this point, however, though I had my suspicions, I begged leave to be excused speaking until I had slept upon it. "Heaven forbid," I said, "that I should expose any man to your Majesty's resentment without cause. The wrath of kings is the forerunner of death."

"I have not heard," the king answered, drily, "that the

Duke of Bouillon has called in a leech yet."

Before retiring I learned that his Majesty had with him a score of light horse, whom La Varenne had requisitioned from Melun, and that some of these had each day awaited him at Malesherbes, and returned with him. Further, that Henry had been in the habit of wearing, when riding back in the evening, a purple cloak over his hunting-suit; a fact well known, I felt sure, to the assassins, who, unseen and in perfect safety, could fire at the exact moment when the cloak obscured the feather, and could then make their escape, secured by the stout wall of box, from immediate pursuit.

I was aroused in the morning by La Varenne coming to my bedside and bidding me hasten to the king. I did so, and found his Majesty already in his boots and walking on the terrace with Coquet, his master of the household, Vitry, La Varenne, and a gentleman unknown to me. On seeing me he dismissed them, and, while I was still a great way off, called out, chiding me for my laziness; then taking me by the hand in the most obliging manner, he made me walk up and down with him, while he told me what further thoughts he had of this affair; and, hiding nothing from me, even as he bade me speak to him whatever I thought without reserve, he required to know whether I suspected that the Entragues family were cognizant of this.

"I cannot say, sire," I answered, prudently.

"But you suspect?"

"In your Majesty's cause I suspect all," I replied.

He sighed, and seeing that my eyes wandered to the group of gentlemen who had betaken themselves to the terrace steps, and were thence watching us, he asked me if I would answer for them. "For Vitry, who sleeps at my feet when I lie alone? For Coquet?"

"For three of them I will, sire," I answered, firmly. "The fourth I do not know."

"He is M. Louis d'Entragues."

"Ah! the count of Auvergne's half-brother?" I muttered. "And lately returned from service in Savoy? I do not know him, your Majesty. I will answer to-morrow."

"And to-day?" the king asked, with impatience.

Thereupon I begged him to act as he had done each day since his arrival at Fontainebleau - to hunt in the morning, to take his midday meal at Malesherbes, to talk to all as if he had no suspicion; only on his return to take any road save that which passed the Rock of the Serpents.

The king turning to rejoin the others, I found that their attention was no longer directed to us, but to a singular figure which had made its appearance on the skirts of the group, and was seemingly prevented from joining it outright only by the evident merriment with which three of the four courtiers regarded it. The fourth, M. d'Entragues, did not seem to be equally diverted with the stranger's quaint appearance, nor did I fail to notice, being at the moment quick to perceive the slightest point in his conduct, that, while the others were nudging one another, his countenance, darkened by an Italian sun, gloomed on the new-comer with an aspect of angry discomfiture. On his side, M. de Boisrose - for he it was, the aged fashion of his dress more conspicuous than ever - stood eyeing the group in mingled pride and resentment, until, aware of his Majesty's approach, and seeing me in intimate converse with him, he joyfully stepped forward, a look of relief taking place of all others on his countenance.

"Ha, well met!" quoth the king in my ear. "It is your friend of yesterday. Now we will have some sport."

Accordingly, the old soldier approaching with many low bows, the king spoke to him graciously, and bade him say what he sought. It happened then as I had expected. Boisrose, after telling the king his name, turned to me and humbly begged that I would explain his complaint, which I consented to do, and did as follows:

"This, sire," I said, gravely, "is an old and brave soldier, who formerly served your Majesty to good purpose in Normandy; but he has been cheated out of the recompense which he there earned by the trickery and chicanery of one of your Majesty's counsellors, the Baron de Rosny."

I could not continue, for the courtiers, on hearing this from my mouth, and on discovering that the stranger's odd appearance was but a prelude to the real diversion, could not restrain their mirth. The king, concealing his own amusement, turned to them with an angry air, and bade them be silent; and the Gascon, encouraged by this, and by the bold manner in which I had stated his grievance, scowled at them gloriously.

"He alleges, sire," I continued, with the same gravity, "that the Baron de Rosny, after promising him the government of Fecamp, bestowed it on another, being bribed to do so, and has besides been guilty of many base acts which make him unworthy of your Majesty's confidence. That, I think, is your complaint, M. de Boisrose?" I concluded, turning to the soldier, whom my deep seriousness so misled that he took up the story, and, pouring out his wrongs, did not fail to threaten to trounce me, or to add that I was a villain!

He might have said more, but at this the courtiers, perceiving that the king broke into a smile, lost all control over themselves, and, giving vent suddenly to loud peals of laughter, clasped one another by the shoulders, and reeled to and fro in an ecstasy of enjoyment. This led the king to give way also, and he laughed heartily, clapping me again and again on the back; so that, in fine, there were only two serious persons present - the poor Boisrose, who took all for lunatics, and myself, who began to think that perhaps the jest had been carried far enough.

My master presently saw this, and, collecting himself, turned to the amazed Gascon.

"Your complaint is one," he said, "which should not be lightly made. Do you know the Baron de Rosny?"

Boisrose, by this time vastly mystified, said he did not.

"Then," said the king, "I will give you an opportunity of becoming acquainted with him. I shall refer your complaint to him, and he will decide upon it. More," he continued, raising his hand for silence as Boisrose, starting forward, would have appealed to him, "I will introduce you to him now. This is the Baron de Rosny."

The old soldier glared at me for a moment with starting eyeballs, and a dreadful despair seemed to settle on his face. He threw himself on his knees before the king.

"Then, sire," said he, in a heartrending voice, "am I ruined! My six children must starve, and my young wife die by the roadside!"

"That," answered the king, gravely, "must be for the Baron de Rosny to decide. I leave you to your audience."

He made a sign to the others, and, followed by them, walked slowly along the terrace; the while Boisrose, who had risen to his feet, stood looking after him like one demented, shaking, and muttering that it was a cruel jest, and that he had bled for the king, and the king made sport of him.

Presently I touched him on the arm.

"Come, have you nothing to say to me, M. de Boisrose?" I asked, quietly. "You are a brave soldier, and have done France service; why then need you fear? The Baron de Rosny is one man, the king's minister is another. It is the latter who speaks to you now. The office of lieutenant-general of the ordnance in Normandy is empty. It is worth twelve thousand livres by the year. I appoint you to it."

He answered that I mocked him, and that he was going mad, so that it was long before I could persuade him that I was in earnest. When I at last succeeded, his gratitude knew no bounds, and he thanked me again and again with the tears running down his face.

"What I have done for you," I said, modestly, "is the reward of your bravery. I ask only that you will not another time think that they who rule kingdoms are as those gay popinjays yonder."

In a transport of delight he reiterated his offers of service, and, feeling sure that I had now gained him completely, I asked him on a sudden where he had seen Louis d'Entragues before. In two words the truth came out. He had observed him on the previous day in conference at the forest inn with the three bullies whom I had remarked there. I was not surprised at this; D'Entragues's near kinship to the Count of Auvergne, and the mingled feelings with which I knew that the family regarded Henry, preparing me to expect treachery in that quarter. Moreover, the nature of the ambush was proof that its author resided in the neighbourhood and was intimately acquainted with the forest. I should have carried this information at once to my master, but I learned that he had already started, and thus baffled, and believing that his affection for Mademoiselle d'Entragues, if not for her sister, would lead him to act with undue leniency, I conceived and arranged a plan of my own.

About noon, therefore, I set out as if for a ride, attended by La Trape only, but at some distance from the palace we were joined by Boisrose, whom I had bidden to be at that point well armed and mounted. Thus reinforced, for the Gascon was still strong, and in courage a Grillon, I proceeded to Malesherbes by a circuitous route which brought me within sight of the gates about the middle of the afternoon. I then halted under cover of the trees, and waited until I saw the king, attended by several ladies and gentlemen, and followed by eight troopers, issue from the chateau. His Majesty was walking, his horse being led behind him; and seeing this I rode out and approached the party as if I had that moment arrived to meet the king.

It would not ill become me on this occasion to make some reflections on the hollowness of court life, which has seldom been better exemplified than in the scene before me. The sun was low, but its warm beams, falling aslant on the gaily dressed group at the gates and on the flowered terraces and gray walls behind them, seemed to present a picture at once peaceful and joyous. Yet I knew that treachery and death were lurking in the midst, and it was only by an effort that, as I rode up, I could make answer to the thousand obliging things with which I was greeted, and of which not the least polite were said by M. d'Entragues and his son. I took pains to observe Mademoiselle Susette, a beautiful girl not out of her teens, but noways comparable, as it seemed to me, in expression and vivacity, with her famous sister. She was walking beside the king, her hands full of flowers, and her face flushed with excitement and timidity, and I came quickly to the conclusion that she knew nothing of what was intended by her family, who, having made the one sister the means of gratifying their avarice, were now baiting the trap of their revenge with the other.

Henry parted from her at length, and mounted his horse amid a ripple of laughter and compliments, D'Entragues holding the stirrup and his son the cloak. I observed that the latter, as I had expected, was prepared to accompany us, which rendered my plan more feasible. Our road lay for a league in the direction of the Rock of the Serpents, the track which passed the latter presently diverging from it. For some distance we rode along in easy talk, but, on approaching the point of separation, the king looked at me with a whimsical air, as though he would lay on me the burden of finding an excuse for avoiding the shorter way home. I had foreseen this, and looked round to ascertain the position of our company. I found that La Varenne and D'Entragues were close behind us, while the troopers, with La Trape and Boisrose, were a hundred paces farther to the rear, and Vitry and Coquet had dropped out of sight. This being so, I suddenly reined in my horse so as to back it into that of D'Entragues, and then wheeled round on the latter, taking care to be between him and the king.

"M. Louis d'Entragues," I said, dropping the mask and addressing him with all the scorn and detestation which I felt, and which he deserved, "your plot is discovered! If you would save your life confess to his Majesty here and now all you know, and throw yourself on his mercy!"

I confess that I had failed to take into account the pitch to which his nerves would be strung at such a time, and had expected to produce a greater effect than followed my words. His hand went indeed to his breast, but it was hard to say which was the more discomposed, La Varenne or he. And the manner in which, with scorn and defiance, he flung back my accusation in my teeth, lacked neither vigour nor the semblance of innocence. While Henry was puzzled, La Varenne was appalled. I saw that I had gone too far, or not far enough, and at once calling into my face and form all the sternness in my power, I bade the traitor remain where he was, then turning to his Majesty I craved leave to speak to him apart.

He hesitated, looking from me to D'Entragues with an air of displeasure which embraced us both, but in the end, without permitting M. Louis to speak, he complied, and, going aside with me, bade me, with coldness, speak out.

As soon, however, as I had repeated to him Boisrose's words, his face underwent a change, for he, too, had remarked the discomfiture which the latter's appearance had caused D'Entragues in the morning.

"Ha! the villain!" he said. "I do not now think you precipitate. Arrest him at once, but do him no harm!"

"If he resist, sire?" I asked.

"He will not," the king answered. "And in no case harm him! You understand me?"

I bowed, having my own thoughts on the subject, and the king, without looking again at D'Entragues, rode quickly away. M. Louis tried to follow, and cried loudly after him, but I thrust my horse in the way, and bade him consider himself a prisoner; at the same time requesting La Varenne, with Vitry and Coquet, who had come up and were looking on like men thunderstruck, to take four of the guards and follow the king.

"Then, sir, what do you intend to do with me?" D'Entragues asked, the air of fierceness with which he looked from me to the six men who remained barely disguising his apprehensions.

"That depends, M. Louis," I replied, recurring to my usual tone of politeness, "on your answers to three questions."

He shrugged his shoulders. "Ask them," he said, curtly.

"Do you deny that you have laid an ambush for the king on the road which passes the Rock of the Serpents?"

"Absolutely."

"Or that you were yesterday at an inn near here in converse with three men?"

"Absolutely."

"Do you deny that there is such an ambush laid?"

"Absolutely," he repeated, with scorn. "It is an old wives' story. I would stake my life on it."

"Enough," I answered, slowly. "You have been your own judge. The evening grows cold, and as you are my prisoner I must have a care of you. Kindly put on this cloak and precede me, M. d'Entragues. We return to Fontainebleau by the Rock of the Serpents."

His eyes meeting mine, it seemed to me that for a second he held his breath and hesitated, while a cold shadow fell and dwelt upon his sallow face. But the stern, gloomy countenances of La Trape and Boisrose, who had ridden up to his rein, and were awaiting his answer with their swords drawn, determined him. With a loud laugh he took the cloak. "It is new, I hope?" he said, lightly, as he threw it over his shoulders.

It was not, and I apologised, adding, however, that no one but the king had worn it. On this he settled it about him; and having heard me strictly charge the two guards who followed with their arquebuses ready, to fire on him should he try to escape, he turned his horse's head into the path and rode slowly along it, while we followed a few paces behind in double file.

The sun had set, and such light as remained fell cold and gray between the trees. The crackling of a stick under a horse's hoof, or the ring of a spur against a scabbard, were the only sounds which broke the stillness of the wood as we proceeded. We had gone some little way when M. Louis halted, and, turning in his saddle, called to me.

"M. de Rosny," he said, - the light had so far failed that I could scarcely see his face, - "I have a meeting with the Viscount de Caylus on Saturday about a little matter of a lady's glove. Should anything prevent my appearance - "

"I will see that a proper explanation is given," I answered, bowing.

"Or if M. d'Entragues will permit me," eagerly exclaimed the Gascon, who was riding by my side, "M. de Boisrose of St. Palais, gently born, through before unknown to him, I will appear in his place and make the Viscount de Caylus swallow the glove."

"You will?" said M. Louis, with politeness. "You are a gentleman. I am obliged to you."

He waved his hand with a gesture which I afterward well remembered, and, giving his horse the rein, went forward along the path at a brisk walk. We followed, and I had just remarked that a plant of box was beginning here and there to take the place of the usual undergrowth, when a sheet of flame seemed to leap out through the dusk to meet him, and, his horse rearing wildly, he fell headlong from the saddle without word or cry. My men would have sprung forward before the noise of the report had died away, and might possibly have overtaken one or more of the assassins; but I restrained them. When La Trape dismounted and raised the fallen man, the latter was dead.

Such were the circumstances, now for the first time made public, which attended the discovery of this, the least known, yet one of the most dangerous, of the many plots which were directed against the life of my master. The course which I adopted may be blamed by some, but it is enough for me that after the lapse of years it is approved by my conscience and by the course of events. For it was ever the misfortune of that great king to treat those with leniency whom no indulgence could win; and I bear with me to this day the bitter assurance that, had the fate which overtook Louis d'Entragues embraced the whole of that family, the blow which ten years later cut short Henry's career would never have been struck.

www.ingramcontent.com/pod-product-compliance
Lightning Source LLC
LaVergne TN
LVHW090955080826
845145LV00003B/1016

* 9 7 8 1 5 9 5 4 0 5 2 8 9 *